Losing CROW

Bloody Saints MC Book 1

Roxanne Greening

Text Copyright 2019 © Roxanne Greening

All Rights Reserved

All rights reserved in all media. No part of this book may be used or reproduced without written permission. Except in the case of brief quotations embodied in critical articles and reviews.

The moral rights of Losing Crow as the author of this work has been asserted by her in accordance with the copyright, designs, and patients act of 1988.

This is a work of fiction. All names, characters, locales, and incidents are the products of the author's imagination and any resemblance to places or events is coincidental or fictionalized.

Published in the United States of America 2019

Dedicated to my husband and kids for their love and support. To my dad and my mom for making me who I am today. And the rest of my family for all their support!

About The Author:

Roxanne Greening is a mother of two young children and lives in the beautiful rural area in West Virginia, USA. It was because of her love for reading romances, that Roxanne decided to write her own. However, it is the MC romances that she enjoys writing the most. "Being able to become a rebel, an outlaw (in fiction) is a powerful thing." And so, Axel, the first book of the SONS OF THE APOCALYPSE, was published in August 2016.

Her comedy nonfiction, The Rantings of a Crazy Person, was born out of demands from her family and friends to write about her own experiences. And her children's book, The chronicles of rocky and binx aka the steam punk kid and the angel of death. Titanic's Doom! Came from wanting to write a book for her son who suffers from ADHD.

Roxanne also enjoys to quilt, and secretly wants to be a ninja.

Prologue:
Three Years Ago.

I should have seen my sister's silent screams for help. She needed me to be there for her years ago, and I had what? Not done enough. I knew the loss of our parents messed her up, but this was becoming too much. Can you save someone who really didn't want to be saved?

I stared at my sister as anger, fear, and shame coursed through me. Shame at my previous feelings. Why couldn't I reach her? Was I not doing enough? I honestly didn't understand why she was doing this. Did she not see how wrong this was?

Once again, I had to come and get her. She had found herself in another shit hole with another abusive man. And here I was pulling her from the fire.

"She's not going anywhere," Raoul snapped at me as he grabbed her arm in what looked like an extremely painful grasp.

"She's coming with me," I tell him firmly.

Terror wanted to take over. Raoul had about hundred pounds maybe more on me, and he was what people called a meathead. The kind of men you found at the gym all beefed up and loaded with steroids.

I wanted to look down and make sure there were no needles around, and tears threatened to fill my eyes. This need for drugs was my sister's way of dealing with our world going sideways.

"The fuck she is," he shouts tugging her closer to him.

Something deep inside me roared and came surging forward. This wasn't the first time that I went toe to toe with a bully. If my sister kept this up, I'm sure it wouldn't be my last.

"Listen, we can do this the easy way or the hard way," I tell him. I kept my tone even when all I wanted to do was grab his head and bash it off the closest wall.

"Funny little girl. What are you going to do, cry all over me?" he laughs heartily.

Sighing, I throw my shoulders back and give him my sweetest smile.

"I know where you live, where you sleep, and where you work out. I can easily slip in and drop a little something into your favorite drink. Maybe even slip a knife between your ribs when you are high and feeling free. Name your poison, Raoul," I tell him with a sickeningly sweet smile.

His face went a little white the more I spoke. I could see the calculations in his eyes. Would she do it? Would she come for me when I was at my lowest? Weakest?

"You don't scare me," he tried to put on a brave face.

"But you should be. You should be very scared of me. You have the only person left in this world that I care about, and she's struggling in your large paw that you call a hand. You hurt her, and I promise you one thing, you won't see me coming," I tell him coldly.

"Little girl, I could snap your neck right now," he tells me.

"You could, and that's why I have put things in place. If they don't hear from me soon, everything will be put in motion the moment my call doesn't come in," I look at my watch. "Only five more minutes and your life will end."

I had given a co-worker a stack of letters. One to the cops telling them where I was going and who I saw if I didn't make it out of here. One to his gym telling them what kind of drugs and other illegal things he was doing in their gym, and then one to his mother telling her all the heartbreaking things he's been doing, including my death or disappearance.

"Oh really?" he laughs again.

"Raoul, did you think I would walk in here without some sort of contingency? How will your mother feel about all the things you've done? The cops will know where I am and with whom? Maybe even the gym you love so much?" I tell him, my tone even.

"Fuck!" he shouts.

I laugh, and it's filled with the anger, sadness, determination, and basically every feeling that's been locked inside me since we lost our parents in that plane crash.

"What do you want? What do I have to do to get you the fuck out of my life?" he asks.

"First, let go of my sister, then we will walk out that door and never see your fucking ugly face again. Otherwise, I will make one of my promises a reality. I will visit you, and you will cease to breathe," I tell him calmly.

"Crazy bitch take the fucking whore," he pushes her in my direction. I watch as she bounces off the wall and crashes to the floor.

Did she land on any of the used needles? Her eyes looked devoid of feelings telling me she was high, again. How many more times will I do this?

As many times as, it took. I told myself that I could never leave her. She was all that I had in this world. My older sister was broken, and she had only one person who gave a shit about her.

Not taking my eyes fully off the dickhead, I pull my sister to her feet. I then walked sideways down the hall and towards the door.

Sunlight burned my eyes as we made our way down the broken steps. Time to make a trip to the hospital for more tests. I hated every one of them. Was she pregnant? Did she have AIDS? Another STD?

"Julie, we can't keep doing this," I tell her as I buckle her into the car. For once she didn't fight me. Instead, she sagged into the seat and stared out the window at nothing.

My heart broke a little more. I dialed Ronnie's number and waited for her to pick up. I then quickly let her know we made it out of there.

She hated when I did this. Ronnie was my only friend, and I cherished her, but this was my sister. I will always help her.

Chapter 1

Maria

Three Weeks Ago.

I stared at my phone and held it tightly in my grip. Again, Julie called crying and begging for help. I looked at Shawn as he shoved his plastic linked rings into his mouth and started gnawing on it.

My heart melted at the sight. I couldn't keep doing this. Shawn needed me more, and I knew this road was never going to end. If for some miracle it did, I knew it was going to end only one way, with my sister dead.

Ronnie was the only person in this world that I had. We met not long after I escaped from my past, as well as Crow, and moved here.

She too was running from something, and I hoped one day she would open up and tell me. I knew from experience that sharing whatever had her changing her whole life wasn't easy to do.

Sighing, I went under my recent calls and pressed on Ronnie's name. I needed her to watch Shawn, and once again go on the hunt for my sister. Yes, she told me where to find her, but that didn't mean it was going to be easy to locate her. Once I did get to the address, I had to get up the courage and walk in.

The idea of going into one of those drug infested places again made my skin crawl. I should be used to wading into the unknown filth to save Julie from another abusive, controlling drug pusher and pimp.

Tears filled my eyes as I remembered the vibrant woman my sister use to be. She was the one person I looked up too. She was my best friend, and I lost her when we lost our parents.

"I need you to watch Shawn," I tell Ronnie when she picked up the phone.

"Again, Maria?" She asked, her tone relaying her feeling on the matter.

"I can't leave her there," I tell her once again. This was an on-going argument between the two of us, but she always came over to help.

"You need to let her go and walk the fuck away before she gets you killed," Ronnie snapped.

It was something I had just been thinking about. Well, more like my sister being the one dying. Never really thought about the danger I had been putting myself in.

"She needs me, Ronnie," I whispered.

"She can't be saved. It's time you just move on. Please do this, if not for yourself, then for Shawn," she tells me, her voice was getting quieter as she lost some of her anger.

It was a low blow, and we both knew it. Just like I knew Ronnie was sorry, not that she would admit to it.

"I'm coming," she sighed when I didn't respond. The line went silent, and I pulled the phone from my ear. Shawn gurgled and cooed, and my heart melted, again.

Ronnie was right. What was I doing? Shawn needed a more stable environment. I was going to end this and give it my all, but when it was over, I was going to give her a choice. Go to rehab and be in our life or refuse and be on her own.

The thought of turning her away, of her not choosing us gutted me. I knew deep down she wouldn't pick us. The hope that she would pick us was a small flame in the darkness of hopelessness.

Chapter 2

Maria

Three Weeks Ago.

The house looked like the roof was ready to cave in at any moment, the door was missing, and a few windows were missing their glass.

The porch steps were sagging, and the railing was split in half. Also, the once yellow wood siding was missing large pieces in random spots.

My nose wrinkled as I walked into the building scanning the floor as I walked. Needles littered the floor along with piss and vomit.

"Julie?" I called out, hoping she could hear me. I hoped she wasn't in a drug induced coma.

Glass clinked somewhere down the hallway. Moving further into the druggie shithole, I scanned the open doorways not finding her.

Something was sinking like a stone in my stomach. The further I went, the deeper it sunk. Julie wasn't here and my eyes watered.

I just wanted to help my sister. I wanted her back in my life, free of this poison she lived with. I reached the back door and sighed.

Just as I turned to go back, I heard the unmistakable sound of a gun cocking. Someone had just slid a bullet into the chamber.

I froze in place, and my ears strained to hear where the noise was coming from. I soon discovered the unmistakable accent had moved closer and closer to me.

"She's not here, she must have slipped out," his heavy accent sent chills down my spine.

"A few others, yes. The sister's nephew… ," he replied to whomever he was talking too. I could tell this guy must have been on the phone.

"Yes, Julie Botchman. Find the sister," he told whomever.

My heart froze, and my hands turned clammy. Oh, God, this guy was talking about my sister. He was also talking about my son. What the fuck did you do Julie?

Looking around the kitchen, I looked for an escape. There was no way that I could open the door and not be heard. Although, the pantry door was opened just enough that I could slip through the crack.

Looking into the dark closet, I took a breath as I slipped in. I resisted the urge to close the door. Quietly, I stepped into the dark interior. I prayed there were no needles, glass, or anything that would make noise.

I had walked maybe six-feet into the dark room when my eyes adjusted to the large space. Shelves lined the walls, and I could see a hole in the plaster under the last shelf on the right. Squatting, I squeezed into the hole and pressed a filthy hand to my mouth.

Tears streamed freely from my eyes as terrified sobs tried to break past my trembling lips. I heard the door creak and watched as a stream of light bounced off the shelves across from me.

When it closed again, and his feet grew quieter, I knew he had moved on. Pulling out my phone I called Ronnie.

"Get Shawn and go to your house now," I whispered fiercely into the phone.

"What's going on, Maria?" She asked, her tone harsh.

"Please, get the fuck out of there, now," I tell her, my voice getting hard and forceful.

"Fuck!" she shouted, "I'm out, see you soon?"

"I'll be there as soon as I can," I tell her, my voice was barely above a whisper.

Putting the phone close to my chest, I took deep long sucks of oxygen into my lungs. My heart was racing at the rate I was sure a racehorse would be proud of.

I had to go back to the apartment and remove all traces of Ronnie. I also needed some of Shawn's and my parent's things. Stuff that I couldn't live without.

After what felt like forever, but I was sure was only fifteen minutes, I crawled out of the hole that I was stuffed in. I then rushed out of the kitchen door.

Slowly, I circled the house and made my way to my car. I was sure to look over my shoulder and keep my eyes on my rearview mirror as I made my way home.

I wasn't sure how long I had, but thankfully I used a fake last name to rent the place we were living. Also, Shawn's last name was not Botchman, it was Crow.

The thought had me relaxing, only a little, into the leather seat. My knuckles unclenched from the steering wheel. It was time to hide again. This was when I should have given up. I should have said no more. But, I couldn't. I needed to know what the fuck was going on and who the fuck had me on their radar.

I knew one thing for sure, whoever the fuck it was, they weren't looking for me to give me some long-lost relatives estate. No, they were killers, and I knew down to the marrow of my bones I was now walking with a target on my back.

Go to him, find him, you know he will save you, my mind whispered. The thought of going to Crow got me even madder. I was already angry at my sister and the motherfuckers out to kill my son and me.

He was my last resort, my Hail Mary, the white flag that needed to be waved before I darkened his doorstep and asked him for a fucking thing.

My hands shook as I thought about Shawn, I should go to him if only to save Shawn. What kind of mother would I be if I didn't go to the one man, I knew would save him?

The kind who doesn't want to take us from the fire into the frying pan. Because Crow was like a bull. He was just as mean, and just as deadly as the man I heard in that house.

Could I even find him? I tried before, but, I wasn't as desperate as I was now. Also, Shawn's life didn't depend on it then.

Chapter 3

Maria

Three Weeks Ago.

Ronnie's little house was white with green shutters with a green porch. My favorite part has always been the white porch swing. It had blue and green polka dot cushions with little green pillows.

I didn't need to live in an apartment. I mean, I had more then enough money to buy a house, but then I would have to sell it if I ever needed to leave. It was also another paper trail, and that would be another thing that would hold me back.

Moving was so common due to my sister. I never thought about having a cozy little house. It was something I had with my parents and Julie.

I pulled into the driveway behind her small, blue compact car. If you could call it a car, the thing was falling apart. Even from here, I could see the muffler hanging down, not completely attached where it was supposed to be.

I had offered to buy her a safer car. I mean she did me loads of favors, but she always would shake her head and tell me she liked her little car.

The door opened before I reached it, and I watched wearily as Ronnie came out and closed the door, leaving it open a crack so we could hear Shawn.

"What the fuck is going on?" She hissed at me.

She had every right to be angry. I had literally called her and made her fucking run like her life depended on it. And it did. Sighing, I rubbed at my eyes.

"I'm sorry, Ronnie," I tell her. The weight of what I went through was crushing me.

"Maria," she said gently, some of her anger was dissipating, and concern started taking its place.

"My sister did something really bad, Ronnie," I whispered as tears filled my eyes. It was time I let Julie go. Shawn needed me more, and I should have done something before it had gotten this bad.

"I don't know what she did, but they're coming for us," I told her as I slouched forward.

"Who's coming for who?" She demanded, her tone left no room for evasiveness.

"I don't know who they are, but I have a feeling its mob related," I tell her sinking on the porch, my legs no longer willing to hold me.

"Who are they coming for?"

I looked up at her as the error of what I allowed happen and of what I walked into came rushing through me. Tiredness suddenly swamped me.

"Shawn and I," I tell her quietly.

"Fuck! What the fuck did she do?" She snarled.

"I don't know," I tell her as a sob broke from my throat.

"We need to go," she tells me while she looked around. The way she was doing it was a bit odd. Almost professional.

"We?'" I asked.

"Yeah, including me," she tells me, looking down at me like I was a moron.

Hell, I was. I let my sister drag me into this shit over and over. Now, I was paying for it with the possible life my son and me.

"Ronnie, you don't need to do this," I tell her.

"The fuck I don't!" She snarled at me.

Maybe she's right. They might connect us to Ronnie, and her life is probably in danger.

"Not because of whatever you're thinking either," she says forcefully.

"I love you, Ronnie," I tell her, as I stand and pull her into a hug. She was my best friend, my confidant, and my sister. Blood doesn't always define a family. Actions and love do.

"Come on, we need to get fucking moving now. The sooner we go, the harder it is to find us," Ronnie said pulling away and dragging me into the house.

We were going to leave her car and take mine. There were dealerships three towns over, and we were going to trade in my car and get one with Shawn's last name.

It was time to hide and this time, instead of looking for a way to save my sister, I needed to find a way to save my son, my friend, and myself.

Go to him, he will save us. No, Crow was the last person I needed to go too. He didn't need this shit coming his way, and I wasn't so sure I could survive seeing the life that he's made for himself.

"We're going to find Crow," Ronnie tells me as if she was reading my thoughts. I shake my head forcefully, that wasn't happening.

"Just get his location, Maria," she said more gently this time.

"I can't do that," I tell her turning onto the highway.

"It's a safety net. Find him, and if shit blows up in our faces, we go to him," she tells me.

It was something I had already thought of. I knew Ronnie was right. Shawn's little giggles in the back cemented it. I would go to him only if there were no other choice.

Chapter 4

Maria

Two Days Ago.

I watched as the man stalked through the grocery store parking lot. We had moved closer to Crow, and he was literally a fifteen-minute drive away.

The guy in the leather jacket and dark jeans wasn't the motorcycle type. No, he was the kind that tried to blend in. I was sure this guy was in the mafia, and it wasn't the first time I've seen him.

They were closing in again. We moved just three days ago, and already they located us. I got into my car and tried to stay calm as I backed out of my parking spot.

We needed to go on the move again, this time closer to Crow. I knew exactly where he was, and it grated like a cheese grater that I needed to go to him. I felt like a bad puppy with my tail tucked between my legs. I only lasted three fucking weeks!

Looking behind me, I made sure I was not being followed and just for an extra safety measure, I made a few odd turns. When I saw nothing out of the ordinary, I went to the hotel.

We had chosen a room on the first floor with both a front door and a sliding glass door around the corner. It was a great layout and helped if there were an opportunity we had to run.

"Let's go," I tell her quickly as I zip up Shawn's bag.

We never unpacked. We always keep our stuff together in case this happens, which has been happening more and more. We needed to get out of here quickly.

Ronnie grabbed Shawn as I grabbed our bags. Leaving the key in the room, I head back to the car. Tears threatened to break free, but I fought them back.

My stubbornness was going to get my son killed. I hated myself for not going to him sooner. I let my feelings cloud my judgment.

"It's time," I tell her.

She sighed and reached over to grab my hand giving it a hard squeeze. The plan was to leave them in the car which was parked across the street. It was hidden enough that if someone looked, you wouldn't really see them through the tinted windows.

"I don't like this, we should go in with you," she tells me.

"I need to do this alone, it's important Ronnie," I tell her quietly.

Chapter 5

Maria

Present Day.

I knew him before today. As a matter of fact, I saved his life. Okay, maybe not saved his life, just his caffeine addiction. It was more like I paid for his coffee and he showed me what it was like to be with a man.

One popped cherry in the back of his blue pickup. Who knew coffee was going to be so expensive? I didn't. Well, it's more the reward that came with meeting Crow. That was his last name, I never learned his first.

I thought I would never see him again. But I do see him every day and put him to bed every night. Well, his double anyway. Our son, Shawn. I was young and stupid and gave away my virginity to a man who couldn't pay for a cup of coffee. Then, I left with a gift that even though times are hard, I wouldn't trade for anything.

It's not the gift that has me standing outside of my car staring at the clubhouse. I was fighting the need to march in there and tell him he was going to help me whether he liked it or not.

Most would run the other way but what choice did I have? They needed me, and I had to do this for them.

This is for the only family I have left, Ronnie and Shawn. My little bundle of havoc that stirs up my days and fills my nights with smiles and cuddles.

No one said raising a kid was easy and absolutely no one said being a single mom was any easier. I know I should have put more effort into finding him years ago, but I let our past keep me away. The memories were both good and bad.

So, who do I run to the moment the big bad invade my life? The one man who could blow it up and laugh while doing it. Well, at least I hoped he wouldn't blow us up. As long as Ronnie and Shawn were a safe distance away. That thought brought a smile to my lips.

Taking a deep breath, I smooth my tight jean skirt and curse myself for not changing into stuff less form fitting. I wasn't here to seduce the man, I was here to beg him to kill a few people, that's all. A few well-placed bullets, maybe an explosion or two, and voila we'll be free! Everyone can go back to whatever they were doing before. Maybe…

Nodding my head, I let my feet carry me to the entrance. Remember, don't demand anything, he owes you nothing. Breathe and smile. No barring of the teeth and no laser eyes or mom face as Ronnie has dubbed it.

The music wasn't as loud as I thought it would be and the clubhouse was much cleaner than anticipated. I felt the eyes roam over my body. The tables were filled with men drinking and women doing things I don't ever want to see again.

I wasn't a prude, but I didn't want to watch others get blow jobs. Let's face it, I don't see how that could look attractive. Dicks weren't pretty. Period.

"Hello, there sweet thing. Why don't you come over here and sit on daddy's lap? Tell me about all the naughty things you'll like to do," a deep voice whispers into my ear. My throat convulses, and I feel a gag coming. Nasty.

I know I should have tried to meet him outside of the clubhouse, but I was desperate, and waiting wasn't my forte. I lean away from his hot breath blowing across my ear and neck and laugh slightly.

Did these lines really work? My eyes took in the scene around me, and I shook my head. Yes, it appears it does.

"I'm looking for someone," I tell the man as I evade his arm.

He wraps it around my shoulder and pulls me in close. His laugh has his chest bouncing and rubbing against my shoulder.

"I've got you, sweet stuff," he tells me in a husky tone as he tries to pull me close, again.

My patience, that I honestly barely have at this point, snaps. I mean, shit, I've been fucking running for my life for the last three fucking weeks. My temper is boiling, and the need to maim this man almost takes over.

"I'm looking for someone, and that sure as fuck isn't you!" I shout.

Fingers wrap into my hair holding me in place. Not hurting, but not allowing me to move.

"You come into our clubhouse and snub your fucking nose? Who the fuck do you think you are?" He snarls at me, and I growl as the anger radiates off him in waves.

I should have, at this point, let reason take me. Calm the situation and find Crow. What I really do is stomp on this assholes foot as I sink my nails into his wrist. My teeth came into play as I made non-successful attempts to bite him. I probably resemble a deranged hungry zombie.

I was beyond angry. I didn't want to be here, but the lives of my best friend and son demand it. They are at this very moment huddled out in the car hoping to stay hidden. The longer I was in here, the more danger they were in. And this prick was putting his hands on me and suggesting nasty shit.

The hand in my hair tightens. I'll be honest it fucking hurt to have a large amount of hair being pulled as someone controls your head movements with said chunk of hair.

"You're lucky I find you cute," the man reeks of alcohol from today and possibly yesterday. Hell, maybe even last week. Who knows when the man last showered.

"Let me go, and I won't kill you?" I make it sound like a question when honestly, he holds all the damn cards. If that didn't chap my ass, grrrr.

"Lincoln, let her the fuck go, now!" I know that voice and all the hairs on my body start to rise as it echoes around the now silent room.

"Crow?" The man holding me says.

"Hands the fuck off or I cut them off," Crow snarls.

He was getting closer. I start to feel bad for the man who called himself daddy, aka Lincoln. I had this uncontrollable condition that contributed to people getting angry. Through no fault of my own, I might point out.

"Crow?" I ask.

Lincoln, aka Daddy, still hadn't let go of my hair and my head was now pointing to the floor. So, I watch as two black booted feet came into my line of sight.

"Lincoln, let her the fuck go, now," Crow demands, his voice is lethal, and it sends a shiver of fear down my spine.

This time I heard the unmistakable sound of a gun being cocked.

"Shit man," Lincoln says releasing my hair and letting me straighten. My hair, newly released, falls into my face, and I sputter in anger as I push it out of my eyes.

Those beautiful green eyes meet mine, and I am transported back in time to the coffee shop, and the moment my life derailed. It was like a train wreck, like watching two trains head for a collision I should have seen coming a mile away, but I was blind to everything but him.

Chapter 6

Maria

Two Years Ago.

The coffee shop was filled with the scent of rich coffee and deliciously baked goods. My stomach growled, and my eyes squinted. I needed my fix, and this line was not moving. It hasn't even gone an inch in the last five minutes.

What was taking the person at the counter so long? I looked behind me and took in the number of people in line. It all but wound out the door. There must have been at least ten of them.

I debated my options. I could get out of line and march up there to find out what was going on. But, I'd lose my spot. I could also stay here and hope the selfish person holding me back from my sweet treat and rich liquid drug of choice would move along.

Another minute passed and my fists clenched. Dammit, I was going to do this. I was going to go up there and move this damn process along. I needed my caffeine!

Taking a deep breath, I stepped out of my coveted spot and moved towards the counter. A few people protested but I just gave them a look of destruction, and they fell silent. I continued on my path since I didn't stop. I gave them the look on the move; I was good like that.

I was maybe three steps away from the front of the line. The man blocking my view of the person holding me up moved, and I got my first glimpse of the annoyingly selfish person holding up the line.

The black leather vest and light blue jeans had my heart beat erratically. It was like it knew that this was a bad idea. Although my brain was like, fuck that, we can take this man.

Sighing, I took the last few steps and waited for him to notice me. If he did, he made no move to show it. He only tightened his shoulders, and his hand gripped the phone to his ear a little tighter.

"Fuck, man, I need like three dollars. Get your ass here now," he barked into the phone.

I should have backed away and gone to the end of the line. Pretend that this man wasn't here and just wait for my fix, like every other person in this place.

I thought of how long I could be waiting and sighed. There was no way I was walking away now. I did give up my spot.

"Excuse me," I said, lower then I planned.

When he didn't even turn and look at me, I rolled my eyes and cleared my throat. Still nothing. That's it, I wasn't letting this go. He was a rude asshole, and I hated rude assholes.

"Hey!" I shouted.

His hand lowered, and the phone disappeared into his pocket. He then turned around and looked down at me. Yes, looked down because he was a giant of a man. Maybe six foot four? Maybe even jolly green giant size.

"Look, Mr. Giant, I need my coffee. I'm late, and you are between me and what I need," I tried to sound rational, but I wasn't so sure I succeeded in that.

"Yeah, me too," he tells me with what suspiciously sounded like laughter in his voice.

"What you need to do is get the hell out of my way." I snarl. Not liking his tone one iota.

"I'm waiting for someone to bring me my wallet, doll," he tells me with a crooked smile.

"How much to get you the fuck out of my way?" I snapped.

I needed my fix, and this man made it sound like it could be forever before I got to it.

"I'm not letting you pay, doll," he tells me firmly.

There he goes using the endearment again. I was no one's doll. Turning I looked at the barista. "How much?"

"Two seventy-three," she sighed.

I wasn't sure if that was relief or annoyance. Now that I thought about it, the barista was batting her nice long fake eyelashes at him. I looked him up and down and took in his dark brown hair, dark green eyes, and tree trunk legs that were encased in perfectly faded jeans. I bet he had a nice six-pack under that t-shirt. Let's not get started on the tattoos on his neck that disappeared into the collar of said shirt.

Yeah, she was annoyed that I was trying to move the hot non - jolly green giant along.

"Here," I tell her with a little more anger then I should have. Shoving the three dollars into her hand.

"Keep the damn change," I tell her with a fake smile.

Her lips turn down in a frown, but her eyes threw daggers in my direction.

"Thanks, doll," he tells me moving aside but not leaving. Maybe I had interrupted some weird courting that I don't think I will ever understand.

I knew one thing, I wasn't going back in line. I was getting what I wanted, and those who didn't like it could kiss my ass.

"Medium hot coffee, triple cream, triple sugar, and one powdered chocolate doughnut. Also, an everything bagel with cream cheese," I tell the now fuming barista.

"You need to get back in line," she snarls at me.

Having had enough bullshit this morning, I place both hands on the counter and lean in like I'm going to tell her a secret.

I make no move to whisper as I tell her, "Get my shit and move the fuck on. If he wants in your pants, he will get there, but right now your job is to get my coffee and food."

I was more hostile than normal. I knew it and couldn't help it. This morning has been nothing but shit. First, my sister Julie stole the rent money and left before I could kick her ass. Then this asshole held up the line, and now this chick was hung up on said man.

Sure, I could dip into my savings again and pay the rent, but it wasn't the point. Julie needs to stay away from the human scum she's been sleeping with. He was going to get her killed. She stole that money again to save his sorry ass. I just knew it.

Loud laughter came from my left. Turning I glared at the man that had made this morning even more intolerable.

I then noticed the man behind me in line had indeed gotten closer to me, and he was not happy that I had cut in front of him.

This wasn't going to be good. I could see it in his eyes. He wasn't one to play nice. This guy was one of those who threw his power around.

Sighing, I kept my eye on the man behind me then turned slightly to the man whose coffee I just paid for.

"Why are you still here?" I asked him.

I was so damn rude, but I couldn't seem to reel it in. His eyes darkened, and his lips twitched.

"Waiting for my wallet, remember?" he said.

My cheeks heated as I remembered that little tidbit. Yeah, I forgot about that. The man in line stepped closer, and I knew he had enough.

"You can't just cut in front of me like that. Do you know who I am?" he snarls.

"Uh, a man waiting for his coffee? And I just made the line move. You're welcome," I tell him.

"You little bitch," he snarls, taking a threating step closer.

He looked like he was going to make a scene in here. Honestly, I thought he was going to try to chase me down with a vengeance once we got outside.

Turning fully to him I tried to muster up a calming sweet smile. I'm pretty sure it looked more like a baring of the teeth with a slight grimace.

"Look, I'm sorry. I'll be out of your way any moment now," I tell him only to realize the barista was still standing there looking at me.

"Move," I shout at her. Seriously, what the fuck?

Her eyes turned to slits. Then her hands balled up, and her mouth pinched together.

"I don't have to listen to you," she tells me.

"Actually, you kind of do. Customers are always right and all," I point out.

I'm starting to feel like the world's biggest asshole. It was like all the nice had been sucked out of me. I wasn't normally so nightmarish.

"I really need that coffee and look at the bright side. The sooner you get rid of us, the sooner you can get back to Mr. Hottie," I point out in the nicest tone I could muster.

She eyed me skeptically like she was trying to decide if she was losing by doing what she was supposed to be doing. I wanted to smile, but I fought it back.

Just as I turned back to the man that I cut in front of, he reached for me. I let out a little yelp as I scrambled backward. I watched in slow motion as Mr. Hottie latched onto the man's arm and twisted it behind his back.

"Apologize for being an asshole," the man demanded lowly as he presses harder on the violent man's arm. He looked ready to dislocate the man's shoulder, and I instantly felt bad for all the trouble I was causing.

"I'm sorry," I tell them all.

"Not you, him," Mr. Hottie said with a deep growl.

"If you think I'm going to, ow, fuck that hurts. I'm sorry," he squeals at the end.

More shame burned into me. I felt like an asshole of epic proportions.

My coffee and food appeared, and I handed her a ten and told her to keep the two-dollar change. I didn't look back as I rushed from the building.

A large calloused hand latched onto my arm and pulled me to a halt just outside the door.

"Wait, I owe you," he tells me.

"You don't owe me anything. You saved me back there," I tell Mr. Hottie.

My eyes go to the shop and the angry people inside. Looks like it's time to find a new place to get my fix. I really liked this place too.

"Then you owe me, let me take you out," he tells me.

I don't think it was really a question, more of a yeah this is happening. Like a fool, I just nodded my head.

"Meet me at the ice cream shop on third?" I ask him.

"Yeah, six tonight," he tells me letting me go and walking towards his bike. The black Harley gleamed in the sunlight.

"Wait!" I shouted.

He turned and looked at me. Something in me warmed under his stare.

"I don't even know your name," I tell him blushing slightly.

"Crow," he tells me with a laugh.

"Crow? For real?" I shout.

"Yeah, Crow," he said it slowly with an undercurrent of amusement.

"I'm Maria," I tell him.

"See you tonight, Maria," he shouts before climbing on his bike and leaving me standing there watching him disappear around a corner and out of sight.

Present day

"Hey," someone snaps their fingers in my face. My cheeks heat with embarrassment as reality comes back to me. I lost myself in the memory at the worst possible time.

I close my eyes and start counting backward from ten. When I get to one, embarrassment and anger are still hard to swallow. I want to scream at the swirl of emotions that are threatening to choke the very life from me.

"Crow," I croak.

I feel a stream of hot air against my face and my eyes open immediately. I see the most intense green eyes. They seem so dark they look almost black. Crow is leaning down and looking at me with the oddest expression. He looks both relieved and irritated.

"I need to talk to you," I tell him when he still hasn't said a word. My fingers twist into each other as I wait for him to say something. I feel oddly disappointed when nothing comes.

Crow looks ready to leave. Like he is just going to walk away without asking what I need and want. Desperation has me reaching for him.

"I need your help," I rush to say. My hands latch onto Crow's arm, gripping it as tight as I can. Considering my fingers are minuscule compared to his, they nowhere near touch each other as they circle his arm. Yes, he is that big.

"Follow me," he growls.

This is not going how I thought it would. Does Crow even remember me? Am I wasting my time? The hope I have been harboring starts to dim.

Chapter 7

Crow

Present Day.

I watch as she sits in the chair in front of my desk and shifts. Crossing one leg over the other and then repeating on the other leg.

It should make me feel good to see her uncomfortable, but it doesn't. Where the fuck has, she been all this time and why the fuck did she leave?

"What can I do for you?" I ask her keeping my tone even.

"I need your help," she tells me swallowing hard.

"So, you've said. What can I do for you?" I ask her.

"I…," she starts.

"Look, I don't have all day. Spit it the fuck out," I snap at her.

I want to grab and pull her into my arms and beg her to never leave me again. But I also want to tell her to get the fuck out and never come back.

"You don't need to be a fucking asshole," she growls at me.

Ah, there's the Maria I know.

"You have some balls walking into my club after what, two fucking years? Asking for my help and calling me an asshole," I tell her coldly.

"You're right, I'm sorry," she tells me, looking anything but sorry.

"Again, what the fuck can I do for you, Maria?" I ask her again.

"This is a mistake," she says while she sighs.

I watch as she climbs to her feet determine to leave. That isn't happening.

"Sit the fuck down," I demand harshly.

Her ass hits the seat before her brain can fully comprehend what her body just did. I can see it written all over her face.

"You must be pretty desperate to come to me. So, what can I do for you?" I ask her, this time trying to keep the anger out of my voice.

"I'm in trouble," she whispers.

Something in me twists. Maria still has that kind of power over me. And I fucking hate it.

"What kind of trouble?" I ask her, my tone smooth.

I want to flip the fucking desk and throw my chair at the wall.

"My sister got herself in deep this time, and they're calling in a blood debt," she tells me quietly.

My blood boils. Blood debts are no fucking joke. Whoever she owes or fucked over is going to stop at nothing until the debt or slight is paid.

They will own Maria. They could kill her, sell her into slavery, keep her and do unimaginable things to her. The moment they call it a blood debt, she is theirs.

"Where's Julie and what the fuck did she get you into this time?" I snap.

"I don't know where she is, she disappeared three weeks ago after she called me for help. I went looking for her, but she was gone," she tells me, her eyes are filled with tears.

"What did she do?" I demand.

"She stole from the Albanians, and I think she killed one of them," she whispers.

"There is no saving your sister Maria. You understand, that right?" I ask her. I should have been more understanding, maybe less cold, but the anger and resentment are easy to hear in my voice.

Chapter 8

Maria

Present Day.

I stare at the man that I love, regardless of our past or the years that have separated us. Anger rises hard and fast, and I stand and lean over the desk getting into his face.

"Listen, you fucking asshole. I won't beg you for a fucking thing. I know my sister is as good as dead, but I have other people to worry about. Not that you give two fucking shits," I scream.

"Calm your ass down and sit the fuck down," he growls.

"You either help me, or you don't, I learned what kind of person you were two years ago. I should know better than to come here," I tell him standing again.

This is a mistake. I fucking hate that I am here and that I have sunk so low and became so desperate.

The mother in me rears her head. I have no one but Ronnie. Although, if I don't make it, I want Shawn to be with his father. Unless Crow doesn't want him, that is.

"I need two things from you Crow. If I don't make it out of this, I need you to take Shawn, and I need you to keep an eye on Ronnie," I tell him, my voice chokes.

"What the fuck are you talking about?" He asks, his tone deadly.

"Our son. I need you to take him and keep him safe. I need you to keep them both safe Ronnie and Shawn," I tell him through the lump clogging my throat.

I have never pictured a day when I would have to leave Shawn. That I won't be there to see him grow. To graduate, get married, and have kids. So many things I won't see. So many times he would need me, and I won't be there.

My feet carried me to the door as my heart shatters into a pile of dust. Saying goodbye is going to be the hardest thing I've ever had to do. But, I need to put space between us now and get as far away from Shawn and Ronnie as I can.

If they find them… I really don't want to think about it. No, when they came for me, I will be alone. All traces of my son will be gone.

My hand latches onto the doorknob. I don't turn and look at Crow as I turn it. There is no need. I said goodbye to him years ago. This is my Hail Mary, my last chance.

Just as the door creaks open, it slams shut. A large hand is keeping it closed and preventing me from opening it.

Chapter 9

Maria

Three Weeks Ago.

Little feet toddled down the hallway followed by childish giggles. Shawn had learned to walk four months ago, one month before he turned one year old.

Since then, he's been hard to keep in one spot. I laugh as he comes barreling into the living room carrying his favorite dinosaur. The little plastic figure was cheap, but you would think it was a rare treasure with how he treats it.

"Ma, ma, ma," he giggled.

Guilt filled me again as it always does when I see his dimpled smile. I should have tried harder to find Crow. But, I didn't know his real name and the only clubhouse that matched the name on his back patch, flat out told me to take a hike when I showed up looking for him.

I hated him even then for making me fall in love. I had foolishly thought we were exclusive, but I couldn't have been more wrong.

Opening my arms, I pick up my son as he launched himself at me. My smile was spread so wide, my face hurt.

He looks so much like Crow. Shawn has dark brown hair which is almost black with dark green eyes. The little dimples are all his thought. I kissed his cheeks and hugged him tightly.

"Mama loves you so much," I tell him.

His arms wrap around me and the little dinosaur digs into my shoulder. My cell phone started to ring, and I sigh in disappointment as I set him back on his feet. I hated putting him down because I knew soon, he wouldn't want to be held.

"Julie?" I ask as I press the green phone icon.

"I messed up," she sobs into my ear.

"Oh no, Julie. What did you do this time?" I ask her, already planning who I needed to call and all the steps I would need to get her out of trouble.

"I stole from someone important, and I think I hurt him," she tells me, her words were confusing and jumbled.

"Who? Julie, who did you steal from?" I would get back to the part where she said she hurt them later. First, I needed to find out who she took, whatever it was, from.

"Albanians," she cried into the phone.

"I don't understand," I tell her.

"This is your fault. If you had just given me the money that I needed, I wouldn't have had to take what I needed from them," Julie lashed out at me.

It clicked into place, and my stomach sank hard. My sister came to me again wanting money so she could get her next fix. This time I didn't give it to her. I kept putting her into rehab, but she would always go back to doing the poison she loves so much.

Giving her the money was so she could eat and survive. Although I knew in some deep part of my brain, that I tried to ignore, she really used it to get high. And still, I gave it to her. What kind of sister was I? I should have cut her off after she blew through her inheritance.

"Oh, god, Julie," I whispered. My stomach was twisting, and my eyes darted to my son who was busy playing with his mega blocks on the floor.

"Give it back," I tell her firmly.

"NO, it's mine!" She shouts.

My hand tightened on the phone. I knew whatever Julie took was expensive. I wasn't sure I could save her this time, especially if she hurt one of them.

"Julie, please," I tried to reason with her, "You need to give it back. You understand that don't you?"

"Come get me, please," she pleads, not responding to anything I've said.

I once again looked at Shawn. I couldn't bring her here, not near him. Shawn didn't need to see Julie like this.

"Where are you?" I asked her.

"Deering Park," she tells me.

"I'm going to call a friend to help with Shawn, and then I'll be there okay? Don't go anywhere, Julie," I tell her.

Instead of responding she hung up. Taking a deep breath, I tried to prepare myself for what was next. Ronnie was going to be angry that I was running to her rescue, again. She will tell me it's time to let her go. Five years of picking Julie up and trying to save her was enough. It's obvious my sister wasn't going to change.

But the same question always comes up. Could I give up on my sister?

You could go to him, Crow will help you. My mind whispered. Just thinking his name transported me back two years ago. To the memories that always haunted me.

Chapter 10

Maria

Two Years Ago.

The air was cooler than it had been thirty minutes ago. I had foolishly left my jacket at home since I was so excited about this date. In my haste, I forgot it but was able to get here almost an hour early.

The ice cream shop was just finishing its happy hour boom when I heard his bike roaring close by. My stomach jumped, and butterflies filled my tummy.

What was I thinking? This man was dangerous, I knew that. It literally radiated off him in waves. The thought of danger brought a little excitement to the evening.

"Ready?" Crow called to me.

My smile stretched over my face, and I remind myself over and over to take it slow and not run. Running would make me look both crazy and desperate. I'll leave that to the second date. That thought made me laugh a little.

Grabbing his outstretched hand, I swung my leg over his bike. I was so cold before, but the heat of his body seemed to shield me from the night air.

I locked my fingers together on his abdomen and fought the sigh that wanted to escape. The man was solid! I could feel the dips and valleys of his muscles through his shirt.

"Where are we going?" I asked, raising my voice to be heard over the rumble of the motor.

"Dinner," he told me.

I waited for him to elaborate but then squealed in the most horrendously, embarrassing way as he roared off at a very high speed, I thought was only possible in the movies. I resisted the urge to look behind me to see if we were being chased.

The ride was peaceful, at least it was after I grew accustomed to the ridiculous speed he was traveling. When we finally stopped, I was a little disappointed. I had no idea a motorcycle could be so liberating.

"Here," he said, holding out his hand to help me climb off my new favorite vehicle. I smiled and tried to keep the shaking, that I had no control over, to a minimum.

I watched the way his jeans stretched a little tighter over his ass as he swung his leg over the bike. His eyes filled with laughter as he caught me checking him out.

Instead of embracing myself I turned and looked at the restaurant we had pulled up too. It was fancier than I had planned for. Looking down at my jeans and then at him I questioned if this place was a good idea. Could he afford this? I knew that I couldn't.

"Ready?" he asked.

I could only nod my head as the worry started to tug at me. Snap out of it, Maria. You said you would be relaxed tonight, not the uptight crazy woman you normally are.

Taking a deep breath, I rolled my shoulders then pasted the biggest, happiest smile on my face. Not that it was difficult since I was the lucky woman out with this hot man.

"Table for two?" The hostess asked with an overly dramatic purr.

I rolled my eyes and sighed. We haven't even made it all the way into the restaurant, and they were trying to get his attention.

"Yes," I tell her with a sweet smile, but my eyes said die, bitch, die. I mean, what the fuck? I was standing right here!

Crow laughed, and I couldn't help but smile. He knew what I was doing just like he knew what she was doing. I'm sure it happens to him all the damn time. For some reason, it irritated me more than it should have.

The waitress wasn't much better. I thought for sure she was going to trip over her feet when she came back to the table with our drinks. Her eyes ate him up like he was the last piece of chocolate cake at the bakery.

This little green monster kept rearing its ugly head every time she leaned over, expertly placing her tits in his face. Like hello, I'm sitting right fucking here.

Not once had he paid her the attention she wanted. He didn't even encourage her bullshit in the slightest bit. But still, when she came back with our bill, her number was at the top of the receipt, the blue ink standing out brightly against the white paper. I had to fight the urge to stab her with the fork still on my plate.

After dinner, he took me home. I expected him to try and get in my pants, but he just walked me to my door and gave me a brief toe-curling kiss. That was the night Crow stole the first piece of my heart.

Chapter 11

Maria

Present Day.

"You better fucking explain yourself, right the fuck now!" he growls in my ear.

I could feel him back up, and his heat was leaving me. The cold was lashing out at me from his icy voice. It burned me, and I could feel the frostbite burning into my skin. I slowly turn and look in his eyes. The anger and resentment hit me in full force. He has no right to be mad at me after everything he did.

"I tried to tell you, even after her," I snarl at him.

"I have a son? And you kept him from me?" he shouts.

I love how he glosses over her. Like he chooses not to hear me. His eyes are dark and are filled with anger. It all sets me on edge making me lash back at him.

"I fucking came here and to the other clubhouse looking for you. I was told they didn't know you!" I shout back.

The memories were haunting me, hurting me, and making me angrier. Crow made me love him then he tore my fucking heart out and stomped on it until it was nothing but mush on the ground. Like baby food smeared all over the concrete sidewalk.

The memories bring me back to the moment that I showed him how much I loved him. It was the day I was sure Shawn was conceived. The day I thought our future was forever intertwined. It still was but not in the way I thought it would be.

Two Years Ago

I've been seeing Crow more and more over the last week and, somehow, someway he burrowed into my chest and had stolen my heart.

Crow's eyes kept straying from the road to take in my bare legs and tight jean skirt. He had my blood rushing faster, heating me to the point I was sure I could heat the truck with my body heat alone.

My underwear dampened to the point they were sticking to me. I wanted this man like I wanted my next breath. Sunlight caressed my skin as we drove to the park. It was a cliff overlooking the city. At this time of day, it would be more than likely deserted.

How was I going to keep myself from throwing all caution to the wind and climbing him like a monkey after its last banana?

His eyes once again looked at my thighs, and his hand tightened on the steering wheel so hard, I feared it might bend under pressure.

There was this insistent throbbing, and I tried so hard to alleviate it by pressing my thighs closer together. I needed Crow so bad. A small amount of fear started to rear its head. I knew it was going to hurt the first time and for so long I pictured losing my virginity in some hotel with roses and candles. Cliché, I know.

I could see the trees parting as we drove further down the dirt road. I was leading us to the spot we had planned for our picnic. Looking at Crow, you would never in a hundred years think he was some romantic. But this little outing was proof of that.

I was so lost in thought that I didn't notice we had parked. Crow had made no move to get out of the car, and confusion had me looking at him. It looked like he was trying to calm down.

Did he feel like I did? This need to straddle him? To feel him deep inside me where no one had ever been before?

"Don't look at me like that, baby," Crow tells me, his voice was low and filled with heat.

I didn't understand what he was talking about. Was I giving him a funny look? Like a silly face or something? Oh, god, did he know I wanted to unzip his dark jeans to see what's hidden behind them?

The thought made me blush. What was wrong with me? I never thought about these things before.

"I don't understand," I tell him truthfully, secretly hoping he would do what I wanted and pull me to him.

"Like you want me to fuck you," Crow growled.

I pressed my thighs harder together and closed my eyes. This need was getting to be too much. More wetness seeped onto my panties making them uncomfortable. I wanted to take them off, maybe when Crow got out I could?

"Fuck!" he groaned.

Before I could think of something to say, or ask if he was alright, he had me in his lap with one leg over each of his thighs. My pussy then pressed firmly into his hard cock.

The pressure had this tingle shooting through me, and I shifted. Oh, that felt good. So, I did it again. This time applying more pressure and settling myself more firmly against Crow.

His lips pressed into my neck, and I shivered at the contact. It only added to the need that seemed to be boiling in my blood.

"If you don't stop this baby, I'm going to pull those panties aside and shove my dick so far into that tight pussy of yours. You will soon feel me in your throat.

The thought of Crow inside me had a moan slip past my parted lips. I shifted again rubbing myself against him and grinding down hard.

I felt his hand on my thighs spreading them further apart, forcing me to sink harder into his lap. My head fell back as his fingers press against my clit.

Another moan tore from my lips, and I cried out in surprise as Crow's long thick digits sunk deep inside me. It was tight, and the stretching hurt.

I wanted to tell Crow that it wasn't going to work when he once again touched my clit. Oh my god, that felt SOOO fucking good.

I let my head fall back again as my hips jerked. I wanted him deeper, I wanted more. I cried out at the loss of his fingers as they slowly left my body only to drive back in.

"Oh god," I screamed.

My hips rotated, and I pushed down further on Crow's fingers. I've never felt anything like this.

"That's it, baby, ride my fingers like you will be riding my cock in a few minutes," he groaned in my ear, "So fucking tight."

My nails sunk into his leather cut as he started to push into me faster. It wasn't enough, I needed more.

"Please," I cried.

"I've got you, sweetheart," Crow told me, his voice husky.

But he didn't, not really. I wanted to shout as those fingers left my body, completely leaving me empty. Then, his fingers were back pulling my underwear aside.

My pussy clenched on nothing, begging for the feeling he was just giving me. Begging to find whatever I had been rushing towards with each thrust of those hard fingers.

Something soft rubbed against my throbbing clit and pleasure coursed through me. That felt, oh god, that felt so fucking good.

My hips rocked forward on its own, and then Crow was filling me. He pulled me down hard onto his cock, splitting me open.

"Oh, fuck, baby," he moaned.

Tears filled my eyes as pain washed over me. It hurt. I put my hands on his shoulders, and I tried to pull myself off him and get him out of me. This was more painful than I thought, and I wanted him out of me, now.

Crow's fingers tightened on my hips as he held me, forcing me to stay still and take all of him in my body.

"Shh, sweetheart. It will only hurt for a minute," he promised.

It felt like hours, not minutes. It burned and stung again, and I was too tired to lift myself off Crow. Then, he let me up, but he stopped me before he fully left my body. That's when he pulled me back down again. One of his hands left my hip and pressed against my clit grinding and rubbing it.

Again, Crow allowed me to rise above him before pulling me back down with one hand still holding my hip. The pain started to dull, and soon I was moaning. My head was thrown back as he placed his hand back on my hips, lifted me and pulling me back down harder and harder. Then faster and faster. Hitting something deep inside of me.

My stomach tightened as the pleasure increased to the point it was almost painful. My hips lowered to meet Crow's, and I thrust down as Crow thrust up into my body. Both of us moaned and strained to get to that place I've never been.

"So, fucking tight," Crow groaned.

Releasing my hips he tugged on my shirt, lifting it as he pulled it from my body tossing it somewhere. I honestly didn't care where it landed, As long as he kept thrusting into my body and his hard cock was deep inside of me.

I felt wet heat surround my beaded nipple and then this sucking sensation. It was like a bomb went off inside of me. I exploded, and wetness coated my thighs.

Crow's hands latched onto my hips forcing me down onto his cock hard. He kept pounding into me harder and faster, dragging out my orgasm and pulling me into another.

"Oh, fuck!" he shouted as he pulled me back down onto him, holding my hips firm to him. Heat filled my pussy as he groaned long and loud against my breast.

I laid my head on Crow's shoulder and fought the need to tell him those three little words. They wanted to rush out of my mouth, but I swallowed them back. It was crazy to feel this way so soon.

Reality came crashing down as Crow's fist slams into the wall. Anger and something I can't decipher shadow his eyes.

I am ashamed to say my nipples are like little pebbles. The memory was so real, it felt like I was reliving it. Like we were back in that truck and back at a time where all was perfect.

Chapter 12

Crow

Present Day.

Her eyes flash with anger and hate towards me. Like I was the one in the wrong like I was the one who fucking ran off and kept my son from her.

I can see she is thinking of something; her eyes are melting and her cheeks flushing. My dick jerks in my jeans, and I fucking hate that she has this hold on me.

My fist hits the wall crushing the drywall under the force, and my hand disappears into the hole I made. I want to tell her to get the fuck out. That whatever shit she has gotten into, she is on her own. Just give me our son, and I will keep him safe.

But the words won't come. The thought of what the Albanians are going to do to her rips me open even more than the fact she kept something so important from me. I never thought she had this kind of spitefulness in her, but I am wrong.

"You fucking left me, remember?" I snarl the question at her.

"I'm very fucking aware that I was the one who left," she snaps back.

"Why the fuck did you leave me?" I couldn't help but ask her. I shouldn't care what she has to say, but I do, god fucking help me I do.

"You know why I left, Crow," she said it quietly, the anger has left her voice, turning it to this low, sad tone.

"I wouldn't ask you if I fucking knew the answer to that, Maria," I'm still lashing out, my anger and bitterness seep from me like a disease.

"I thought it was going to be forever Crow. That you were it for me," she sighs walking to the chair and sinks down. She is looking defeated.

Pleasure should be what I feel when I look at her, but instead, I feel this gut-wrenching pain. It hurts to see her like this, and that has some of my anger returning.

Circling around the desk, I stare into her eyes. The tears brimming are like a slap to the face. Fuck her pain. She tore my fucking heart out and kept my kid from me.

"What the fuck happened then, huh?" I ask her coldly.

"What ended it? What had me running from you?" she asks the questions, but her tone said she isn't looking for a response.

She looks like she is remembering it and lost in her thoughts. I don't think she is going to tell me, but she does, and my gut sinks with every word.

Chapter 13

Maria

Two Years ago.

There was this happiness that I felt, and I couldn't contain it. Three weeks with Crow and everything was absolutely perfect. I had been feeling under the weather lately. This stomach bug didn't want to be shaken.

I walked to the pharmacy a block away. It seemed like a good idea. I could have driven, but I was hoping the fresh air would help, maybe in some small way.

Crow wanted to come over and watch movies with me. To take care of me, but I had laughed and told him I didn't want him to catch what I had. I told him that I would be fine. I was going to be spending most of my time sleeping anyway as I was tired as fuck lately.

Being sick seemed to zap the life from you. I knew sleep was one of the best remedies. As I walked, the wind caressed my face blowing hair behind me. I smiled at the thought. The feeling of it hitting my body gently after being holed up in my apartment for the last two days was amazing.

I rounded the corner, and my eyes were drawn to the bike I could see three buildings away. I knew that bike, just like I knew the man leaning against it.

I didn't know the redhead standing between his spread feet. Yes, there was some distance between them. She wasn't exactly close enough to be completely touching, but the fact she was between his legs spoke volumes.

It was intimate no matter how I tried to rationalize the view. There was no way to make what I was seeing say anything but intimacy. They knew each other well, I could see it in the way she laughed, and he reached out to put her hair behind her ear.

The smile on his face had the tears that were in my eyes, spill over. I felt the world crashing down on me. I never thought I would see this. Never thought I was going to do what I did next.

I turned from them. After watching Crow with the girl for what felt like forever. I walked back to my apartment. I didn't think as I grabbed the bag from under my bed.

I was leaving this place and leaving him behind. It was time to move on. I knew if I didn't, I would try to forget what I had seen with my very own eyes. I would try to move forward with Crow like she never existed. I loved him that much and love made you blind. It made you want to forgive and forget.

I wasn't the woman to do that. I deserved better than a cheater. I deserved better then what he was doing to me. A small part of me asked if moving and starting over was a little bit irrational?

Maybe it was, but I didn't care. It wasn't like this place held any real meaning. There was no one here I would miss. I haven't been here long enough to make any attachments.

If not for the life insurance policy my parents left my sister and me, this move wouldn't have been possible. More sadness weighed me down.

Julie had fallen to pieces after we lost them. I had tried to bring her back to the land of the living, but she started to self-medicate with illegal drugs. There was no bringing her back. But I haven't given up not once, and I wouldn't.

Looking around the little place that I called home, I sighed. I have been moving from one place to another. I always stayed close to my sister, maybe a few cities away.

I will have the movers come tomorrow, they were always prompt. Pulling out my phone, I made the call. I needed to get out of here before he came back looking for me.

Once all my clothes were packed, I walked to the door opening and closing it without once looking back. I was going to find a hotel, but first I will find a storage place for the rest of my stuff. All of it was replaceable.

I packed what I wanted in the few bags I had. The photos of my family and the small mementos were all I carried with me.

I still had all of our stuff. The house we lived in was like a museum, a memorial to them. Everything was still in the same place it was when we left. I haven't had the heart to pack it up or sell the place.

Tossing my bags in the back seat, I climbed into the driver's seat and started my car. The radio was off, and the silence cut me.

I was leaving again, but this time I was leaving with another loss etched into my soul. Another crack in my heart.

I thought we were made for each other. That we were meant to be. Soulmates. Another tear fell from my burning eyes.

It was time to start another chapter in my life. A chapter without him. Without everything, I thought I had found.

Present Day

"I foolishly thought I made a clean break. I found out about Shawn about three weeks later. I had sunk into a depression and thought the sickness was from the memories of you and her. Basically, the loss of what I thought we had kept me in this deep hole," sighing I look at Crow, "I came looking for you. I tried both Bloody Saints clubhouses, and no one would tell me where you were. Hell, one of them told me they didn't even know who you were. That no one by that name was a member."

His eyes were hard, not once softening. I had just gutted myself again. Living the second worst moment in my life and he didn't even show a sign he cared.

"What would you have had me do? I didn't even know where you lived!" I shout.

My anger at him is making me lash out. I fucking hate him. I hate him for making me love him, for making me believe I had finally found a home again only to rip it out from under me.

"Who?" he demands.

"Who what?" I ask him in confusion.

"Who told you I wasn't a member?" he demands coldly.

"I don't fucking know. It's not like I asked for his damn name!" I snap.

Out of all of this, he only wants to know who the fuck sent me packing a second time? Seriously?

"Is that all you have to fucking say?" I ask him, my tone turning frosty.

"I have no fucking clue what the fuck you are talking about. Honestly one minute you were here the next you were gone. I spent a whole fucking year looking for you!" Crow growls.

"I didn't imagine the redhead, Crow," I growl back.

He sits there staring at me. Like he's trying to pull back the layers to see all my secrets. I could also see him trying to place what I told him. My fist clench, was there that many fucking redheads in his life that he couldn't remember one goddamn moment?

"Larissa," he sighs.

So, she had a name, other than a man stealing whore. Huh, who knew?

"She was a friend," he tells me.

"A friend you fucked, I'm not stupid, Crow," I tell him coldly.

"I wasn't a fucking choir boy, Maria, so, yes, I fucked her more than once. Is that what you want to hear?" His tone is frigid.

I can't look him in the eye as his words lash at me. It tears a piece of something deep inside of me. I hate he still has the power to hurt me.

"My question is why the fuck didn't you say something? Instead, you ran, why?" Those aren't real questions, they are demands.

My eyes stayed locked on the floor. It was a question even Ronnie had asked me more than once. Why didn't I get up in his face and demand a fucking answer for what I was witnessing? Sometimes I even asked myself that. It's not like I was shy when it came to confrontations.

"Where are they?" he asks, changing tactics.

"Are you going to help us?" I ask him, instead of answering.

"I will, but you will owe me," he tells me coldly.

"Owe you what?" I ask him. I will not blindly agree to something that could potentially take me from our son.

"Something of my choosing," he shrugs.

"It can't involve Shawn," I tell him.

"No, it will be something from you and only you," he replies.

For a moment I thought about walking away. But I ran out of options days ago. Nodding, I keep my eyes on the floor. What's going to happen now?

"Where are they, Maria?" He demands gently.

"Outside," I whisper.

"Go get them," he tells me firmly.

"No, not with that shit going on out there. Shawn doesn't need to see that," the fight in me returns.

"I'll get it fucking cleaned up. Go get my son," he growls.

Standing I turn away, but before I make it to the door, I answer his question. The same question I have refused to answer even to myself.

"I was afraid that it had all been a lie. That you would want the redhead more than me, that I wasn't enough," I tell Crow as I pull open the door.

He doesn't say anything, and I keep walking. They say the truth will set you free, but sometimes it only takes you deeper into hell.

Chapter 14

Crow

Present Day.

I watch as the door closes quietly behind Maria. Her words swirl around me. Fuck! This is a fucking nightmare. Albanians, my son, her friend, and Maria.

I pull my phone from my pocket and quickly text Gage. My grip on the phone is tight, and I can hear it creak under pressure.

Me: Follow her.

Gage: The chick from earlier?

Me: Yes. Follow her. Don't let her the fuck out of your sight.

I had no fucking clue what I wanted from her. Anger and hatred are the only things that I can feel. Maria kept my fucking son from me. She left me and didn't look back.

My fists clench in anger at the thought of what was coming. I need to stop the fucking party out there and have a meeting with my brothers about what was coming.

I slam my hands on the desk and swipe its contents onto the floor. I resist the urge to throw my chair through the wall. Instead, I walk to the door and open it.

Music, grunts, groans and other shit tell me exactly what the fuck is happening out there. The same shit that was happening when I fucking walked back into the office earlier.

Tracy comes sauntering over running her finger down my chest. Just minutes ago, I was sure that my dick was going to be sinking deep inside of her. Then Maria walked through the door. Fucking blowing up my world all over again.

"Clean this shit up and take it to the back rooms!" I shout looking to Weston and moving my finger over my throat telling them to cut the fucking music.

Everyone stops and looks at me. Yeah, this shit is crazy and totally out of character for me. Another rush of anger hits when no one moves.

"Fucking Move!" I command.

I watch as my brothers put on their clothes. The bitches just smile and don't even adjusting a damn thing. My eyes narrow.

"Put your fucking clothes on or get the fuck out of my club," I snarl.

That had them moving. The girls start tugging on shirts and skirts if you could call them that. I pinch the bridge of my nose and apply more and more pressure.

I grab Tracy's hand and drag her closer to my chest. Her giggle is husky from all the smoking she does. Just as I lean down to tell her not to go far, the door opens, and Maria walks in.

Her eyes lock on Tracy and me before she looks towards the floor. Her feet stop moving, and her arms go around her waist. I feel a small amount of pleasure at the thought that I hurt her. It makes me smile, but it is accompanied by an ache in my chest in the same place my heart had died two years ago.

Another chick comes up from behind her and nudges Maria forward while whispering into her ear. I watch as she turns and pulls my son from the girl's hip.

Maria stands sideways and steps forward keeping my son behind them. He has dark hair and tan skin, and it's the first things I notice.

"Later," I tell Tracy and walk towards my son. His big eyes look around the room curiously. The closer I get to him the more I can see his features. His dark green eyes look at me, and something in me twists.

My son looks like me. Almost an exact replica. His smile lights up his face, and it shows a little dimple on the right side of his cheek.

I want to pull him into my arms. I want to hug them both. Maria shifts and my eyes go to her. She looks sad, terrified even.

Actually, she looks gutted and lost, just like I did. I watch as Maria looks over my shoulder and then presses her face into my son's head.

I feel a hand caress my shoulder, and I know it is Tracy. It is a sick satisfaction that hits me. Maria is hurting. Then again, my stomach twists knowing that I am hurting her.

Turning I look at Tracy and tilt my head trying to tell her silently to get the fuck out of here. Her eyes flash at Maria, but then her lips curl into a smile telling me that Maria is once again looking at us.

Instead of focusing on Maria and our son, I watch Tracy's hips sway as she leaves. My dick that was once hard for Tracy is now unaffected by the show.

"I need to clean him up and feed him," Maria says, her voice barely above a whisper.

"You can use my room," I tell her.

"No," she replies, her voice cold.

"What the fuck do you mean no?" I turn back to her.

"I want my own space, not where you and your girlfriend sleep," she sighs, her shoulders slumping.

"Hey, it's okay," the chick with her tells Maria.

I don't respond. What the fuck is there to say? She ripped my insides out when she left me. She. Left. Me. I should correct her that there has been no girlfriend since her. Only quick fucks.

But I don't. I let Maria think what she wants, knowing it was hurting her. I reach for my son and pull him into my arms. Maria releases him without so much as a fight.

His little arms wrap around me before he tugs on my ear. Giggles erupt from him as he pulls on it. My eyes stay glued to his face, taking in every detail.

"I'll have one of the girls make you something to eat," I tell her.

"I need to clean him up," she tells me, her voice devoid of feeling.

I don't want to give him back. I want to hold him close to me and hear his laughs and watch his eyes as they take in the world around him. Instead, I release him and signal for them to follow me.

I was going to put her in the room next to mine. Call it a sick pleasure knowing she is close. She would be able to hear everything I do.

Another sharp pain pierces my chest. I am an asshole. I should put her further away, at least give her a few walls between us. But the thought of her having more than one wall separating us is more than I can handle.

I am fucked up.

Chapter 15

Maria

Present Day.

"What a fucking prick," Ronnie snarls at the closed door.

I fight the tears that want to fall from my stinging eyes. The way the woman was draping herself all over Crow and her smile as she looked at me just made me sad. I blink and think that it's over and has been over for two years. Of course, he will move on.

"Let it go," I tell her laying Shawn down on the bed. He needs a diaper change and some food.

"Did he need to rub that shit in your face?" Ronnie snaps, her cold eyes are still on the door.

"It's been two years, Ronnie," I remind her.

"Yeah and not once have you looked at another man," she points out.

"Crow was and always will be the one for me," I tell her, my eyes staring at my son.

"When this shit is over, we need to find you a man," she says as if I didn't just say anything.

"Ronnie…" I start.

"No, he's moved on, don't you see that? It's time for you to move on as well, Maria. You deserve to be loved," she points out, her voice becomes gentle at the end.

"I am loved by this special little boy right here," I remind her as I press my lips to Shawn's little belly and blow a raspberry. His feet kick as he laughs.

"You know what I mean, so don't play games," Ronnie sighs.

"I'm not playing games. It's been two years, but I left Crow. Yes, it fucking fillets me to see and witness what time has done. But, its over and there is no going back," I say quietly.

Life has moved on, and I stay in this bubble that Crow and I have created together. My love for him never falters. I can see now that it was one-sided.

"I need to feed Shawn, and I don't want to talk about this anymore," I tell her as I pick Shawn up off the bed.

Ronnie opens the door and walks through it. I could see it on her face, she isn't letting this go. My hands shake slightly as I pulled Shawn into my arms.

"Just promise me, when this is over, and we leave this place, that you will try to find someone," I close my eyes and tilt my head back, but I don't respond.

There is no one waiting outside the door to show us where the kitchen is. So instead, we retrace our steps back to the room we came from.

The scent of delicious food pulls me to the left and into an open doorway. Shit! That chick is here, looking as if she is waiting for me.

Her smile is big, cocky even. I want to look away from her, but instead, I keep my eyes level with hers. I am not backing down.

Sure, I am running for my life, but those fuckers are terrifying. This bitch, she has nothing on the people I've have had to go toe to toe with to save my sister.

"Cute kid," she says, her voice holds nothing of the sweetness that normally accompanies those words.

"Stay the fuck away from him," the voice is cold and dark, and it makes me love my best friend even more.

"Look, I just want to feed my son," I try to be diplomatic.

"Crow's mine now. You may have his son, but I'll be having all of his future children," she tells me, her tone cold.

My kid is going to be swearing soon if people keep this shit up. Not that I'm any better, but still.

"I don't want to cause any trouble. I just want to get something for my kid to eat," I tell her again, trying to keep calm.

"I want you gone, bitch," she snarls at me.

I smile, and it stretches across my face. I watch as the bitch looks at me with confusion in her eyes. Shit, I would be confused as well if I was basically trying to bully someone, but instead of leaving, they smile.

Ronnie laughs, "Shit, just got real."

This chick may have Crow now, and she may run the fucking show. But no one stops me from taking care of my kid. No. One.

"I'm going to give you two minutes to get the fuck out of my way," I tell her calmly.

She looks at me like I grew another head. Her eyes dart back and forth between me and Ronnie who is still holding my son.

"You can't tell me what the fuck to do!" she shouts.

"One minute," I tell her.

"If I were you, I would go now," Ronnie says, with glee in her voice.

"You think you can take me?" she snarls at me.

My smile grows wider when her time is up. I don't warn her again, I don't even say a fucking word. I just take a little step closer. I have had it with this bullshit.

It feels like life just keeps kicking me in the lady balls over and over. I am so damn tired of this shit.

My hand shoots out and tangles into her hair. I don't even pause for a dramatic effect. I don't give her a chance to claw at my hand. Nope! I lift my knee and bounce her fucking face off it. I let her go the moment her head whips back from the force. When she crumples to the floor holding her nose, I step over her.

Shawn giggles as the bitch on the floor starts crying. I turn and look at Ronnie. She is tickling his sides. She is also watching the girl on the floor with utter fascination.

"I love you. If we did swing the other way, I would so marry you," she tells me.

I laugh as I grab a paper plate and start tearing up some pancakes for Shawn. The girl is still crying telling me I broke her nose. She continues to talk asking how I am going to pay for this and blah blah blah. I don't give a fucking shit, I warned her ass to get the fuck out of my way.

Chapter 16

Maria

Present Day.

Crow is standing on the other side of my bedroom door. His eyes are dark as he looks down at me. Anger radiates off of him in waves.

I sigh and look up at him. He must be here about his girlfriend. I try to convey with my eyes that I want him to get whatever the fuck he wants to say out and then go the fuck away.

"What the fuck happened?" he growls.

I sigh and give a shrug. I don't really need to tell Crow, I'm sure he already knows.

"Tracy's nose is fucking broken," he tells me, his eyes roam over my face.

What is he looking for? Proof that we got into some girl fight? Yeah, it was a big fight. Her face hit my knee and then she fell on the floor. That was one hell of a vicious catfight. I want to laugh at the thought.

"Should have sold tickets," I grumble.

Yeah, but then she would have had to do something other than cry and bleed all over the place.

"Honestly, Crow it's none of your business," I tell him quietly because it is the truth. It's a fight between two women. Period.

Sighing, he runs his hand over his head. It as a sign that he's frustrated. And I almost smile. There once was a time that I would've grabbed his face between my hands and kissed the frown he had away. Kissed the frustration right out of him.

But those times are long gone. The reminder has me rubbing my face. Why the fuck is he still standing here?

"Can I help you with something else? Or do you mind if I take a nap?" I ask him frustrated.

Ronnie is sitting on the floor playing with Shawn. His favorite dinosaur is clutched in one hand, and the mega blocks are spread out in front of him.

She has agreed to watch him so I can get some rest. I haven't slept in almost two days. Fear of them getting Shawn has kept me up pacing and watching him.

"I want to spend some time with my son," he finally tells me.

"I'll bring Shawn out in a bit," I tell him tiredly.

"No, now," he tells me firmly.

"I've got this," Ronnie tells me while climbing to her feet.

"I don't need a god damn babysitter," he snarls.

"Yeah, big guy, you do," she tells him with a shrug as she pulls Shawn up off the floor.

He looks at me with anger darkening his eyes to an almost black color. My heart lurches. Because under that anger I can see the hurt and pain.

"I know you don't need a babysitter Crow, but it will help Shawn grow accustomed to his new surroundings. This has been hard, to say the least, for the last few weeks," I try to keep my tone gentle.

I need him to understand what I am saying. I don't want to hurt him, even though I have, and I keep doing it. God, why do I care so much?

"Whose fault is that?" He asks me, his tone is harsh and biting.

"Please, I haven't slept in two days. I understand you want to kill me Crow and that you hate me. But, I need sleep, please," I beg him.

It hurts my pride to once again beg him for something. But after our talk in his office, I question who's fault all this really is. Had I walked up to him and talked to him, would things be different now?

God, the what ifs are tearing me apart. His eyes scan my face taking in the dark smudges under my eyes. I have stress lines around my mouth, and I expect him to continue to fight me. But instead, he gives in with a nod. A small truce for now, anyway. The bed is calling my name, and I don't want to go to it. Deep down I am terrified of what waits for me in the dark abyss.

Crow reaches out for Shawn as Ronnie closes the space between them. Stepping back, I watch as she releases Shawn to his father.

"It will be okay," she whispers to me before turning to follow them out of the room.

My question, the one I didn't ask, is if it really was?

Climbing onto the bed, I curl in on myself. My mind fighting with my body. Both knowing I need rest but not wanting to face what awaits me behind my closed eyes.

I was back in this clubhouse two years ago. Back when I was looking for Crow, and a small amount of hope was in my chest, blossoming like a little flower.

It was stolen from me by the man who had his hand in my hair. He started caressing the back of my head. I looked up at the man holding me. His cocky smile clawed at my insides, and it festered like an infected boil. "Crow? Don't know anyone by that name," he laughs.

I wanted to kick him in the balls, he made my skin crawl.

"You in need of a man babe? Come see daddy," Lincoln tells me. Fuck! It was Lincoln, that son of a bitch.

I needed to tell Crow. There was something about him that wasn't right. Why would he lie?

The dream changed pulling me deeper into sleep locking me in a new form of hell.

They found me. Shawn was laying in his pack n play gurgling and cooing up at the ceiling unaware of the men pointing a gun at my head.

"Don't kill them," a cold voice comes from somewhere in the house.

"I have a buyer for them both," the Albanian smiled as the man's voice carried to me. Chills raced over my body. I failed. I couldn't save us.

I could see Ronnie's feet out of the corner of my eye. She had fought them back trying to give me a chance to get Shawn, but another came from the kitchen blocking my exit.

I heard the sound of the gun going off and hitting Ronnie. Her body fell to the floor and the thump it made haunted me. I stared into the cold dead eyes of the man who just killed her.

"You think you could run? That we will not find you?" His laugh was rusty.

"Please, don't do this. I didn't have anything to do with what Julie did. I swear," I beg, my eyes pleading to let me save my son.

"Julie stole my shipment and killed my man," he snarled at me as he leaned in closer. Those dark orbs promise pain and a life I would rather die than live through.

"But you catch a good price. Actually, more than the shipment was worth," he said, his voice was filled with excitement.

I screamed as I fought. I fought to escape, and I fought to save my son. Then hands wrapped around my throat and it cut off my air supply.

There was this dimness, a blackness closing in on me. "Don't worry, I will not kill you," the man smiled cruelly. My eyes stay glued to my son. I watched as one of them picked him up and smiled just before the lights went out.

"Shawn," I scream and sit up.

Hands grip me, pulling me into arms that are familiar. Ronnie's scent starts to fill my nose.

"What the fuck is wrong with her?" Crow demands from somewhere close by.

"Like I told you when you tried to pick her up. She's in hell," Ronnie snarls at him.

"Oh, god! You're alive," I cry into her shoulder.

A small amount of disappointment fills me. I wish it were Crow that was holding me. Soothing me. God save me, but I needed him. I loved him.

"What happened," Ronnie asks, her tone is low and soothing.

"They found us. I tried to save him, I couldn't save us," I whisper pressing both hands to my face. Even now, I'm awake knowing it wasn't real, but the fear and the hopelessness still cling to me.

"It's over, it was a dream," Ronnie tries to comfort me.

"They got so close," I whisper, knowing that if they had gotten us that it was my fault. That I am too prideful to do what I should have done.

"You did the right thing. You're safe now. We're safe now," Ronnie tries again.

"They won't stop until they have me," I tell her. It is the truth. They are going to keep coming. Crow will only do so much. How many lives will I risk to keep mine?

"If I leave, they'll stop. Shawn will then be safe," I say out loud.

"The fuck you will!" Crow shouts.

My eyes dart to his, and the anger and pain tear me apart. I never meant to say it aloud. I know deep inside that he won't let me leave. But, I know it is only a matter of time before they find us.

Is my life worth my sons? No, he will always come first. There is going to come a time when I have to leave. I can see it on Ronnie's face. She knows it too.

It was both terrifying and liberating to know your days are numbered. Doing what I need to do will be so much easier knowing Shawn has his father. That he will be loved and safe.

I only hope one day he will forgive me for what I have to do. That he will understand that I did everything out of love. This won't be the first time I found myself in hell. I didn't meet Ronnie until five months after I ran. And in those five months, I wished for death.

The way Ronnie is looking at me, she knows exactly what I am remembering. She remembers our first encounter just as much as I am.

Sometimes people know what it is like to be trapped. To live through something worse than death and come out on the other side alive, but not whole.

Chapter 17

Crow

Present Day.

Her screams had ripped into me. The way Ronnie seemed unsurprised by them sent a red flag through me. Something happened over the two years she was gone, something that scared her.

Why the fuck do you care? Fuck! I was letting her get under my skin. Right now, I want to keep her at arm's length. I want to keep my anger, disgust, and hate.

I turn and walk down the hallway carrying my son in my arms. His little face is scrunched up as little cries of distress echoes off the walls.

He is feeding off her fears. It guts me to hear him cry and see his tears. I stop and contemplate taking him back to Maria. He needs her because he doesn't fucking know who I am.

Again, another round of anger rushes through me. Instead of continuing, I walk back to Maria's room. I hate that Shawn doesn't know me, but he needs his mother right now.

"Were you back there?" I hear Ronnie's voice carry down the hallway.

"No, it was different this time. They found us," Maria replies, her voice fills with fear.

"You got away," Ronnie tells her soothingly.

"It isn't that, this time it was the Albanians. They killed you and had Shawn," Maria said quietly.

I was standing close to the door rubbing Shawn's back as he quietly laid his head on my shoulder.

"Sometimes I still feel the cold, the pain…" Maria's voice is low and filled with pain.

"You're free, you got away. Don't go back there. You've made it this far, the nightmares have gotten less and less," Ronnie tells her, her voice sounds gentle as if she is trying to soothe a wounded animal.

"I know I'm free, but they keep coming for me in my dreams. Is it sad that I was thankful that it was different this time? That it wasn't….. them," Maria whispers.

"Stop, it's over. Take a deep breath. Shawn is safe. Let that be enough, for now," Ronnie reminds her.

What the fuck is she talking about? Something in my gut twists. What is she hiding from?

"Where do you want him?" I ask as I come into the room. It's apparent they aren't going to continue whatever they were talking about.

"Here," Maria slides over a little and pats the spot she just vacated. She doesn't look at me, she keeps her eyes glued to the floor.

Laying him down, I look at Ronnie. She has the answers that I need, and she is going to spill them one way or another.

Chapter 18

Maria

Present Day.

Ronnie is sitting with Shawn as I venture out of the room. After laying there trying to fight off the panic, the memories try to surface, and I let the hours pass in silence.

Hunger has me coming out of my room, my haven, and my prison. Loud voices are laughing, and the smell of cigarettes fill my nose the closer I get to the main room.

I don't look around, I just keep my head down and continue towards the kitchen. Pans clink together, and laughter fills the room.

Looking up, I half expect to see Tracy only to find the room filled with women wearing more clothing. Sighing, I open the fridge and pull out a beer. Popping the top, I take a long pull. The bitter liquid caresses my tongue before sliding down my throat.

"Whoa, slow it down there," one of the women laughs.

Lowering the bottle, I look at her. Why the fuck does she care if I drink my weight in alcohol? Shit, that's exactly what I need to do.

"I'm Alanna, and these bitches are Brittney, Tori, Cassie, and Bianca," she points to the blond first, then a dark-haired girl who looks like her sister, and then another blond with curls before finally pointing at a woman with dark hair.

I give them a nod and take another deep pull from my beer. Why the fuck do I care who they are? They all wear jeans and a t-shirt. Way more than Tracy, who has worn a nothing skirt, which I think was originally a tube top that she put around her waist. I'm guessing the tank is missing about seven inches of the shirt, as it stops right below her boobs.

"You must be Maria," Cassie says.

I give her a thumbs up still taking long pulls from the bottle.

"You really Crow's old lady?" The one they call Brittney asks.

A frown forms between my eyebrows, do I look fucking old?

"I'm Crow's nothing," I tell them with a bite in my voice.

They all laugh and nod, but I still don't get it, and I hate being the butt end of someone's joke. My glare turns frosty as I stare the women down.

"Respect," Tori holds up her hands with a warm smile.

I still don't relax. I'm already sick of the bitches in this club.

"Look, we mean no disrespect," Alanna says diplomatically.

"It's just that it's obvious you aren't like those bitches out there," Cassie's says with a wicked smile.

"Got to ask, did you really break Tracy's nose?" Bianca asks.

"Fuck, yeah, I did. And I'll do it again and again to the stupid bitch," I snarl.

The beer is now empty, and I definitely need another one. Reaching into the fridge, I pull out another beer. I place the edge of the metal cap against the counter and slam my hand down and smile with satisfaction at the pop. It is followed by the clicking of a metal cap which is bouncing off somewhere.

"I think you just became my new best friend," Bianca says with a laugh.

"Fuck you, bitch," Alanna laughs.

Something in me dislodges, and I smile.

"We're old ladies," Cassis tells me with a smile.

My face must have shown my confusion. None of them are old.

"It's a term of endearment, like saying I'm a wife in their world. I'm the property of Gunner," Cassie's says pointing at herself.

Property? Being called an old lady was an endearment? What the fuck?

"I'm Reyes' property," Alanna says with a smile.

"I'm Ryan's property," Bianca says.

"I'm Zane's property," Tori laughs.

"I'm Topher's property," Brittney says with a wistful sigh.

I still don't get it. Property? Who the fuck wants to be owned by someone?

"Did they buy you?" I ask horrified.

"What? No!" They all shout in unison.

I watch as they turn to each other and laugh. Yeah, five women saying the same thing at the same time is odd as fuck. And apparently, they find it funny.

"Look, I just want to drink a few beers, watch the world blur, and let the fuck go," I tell them all.

I just want to be left the fuck alone. The memories are coming for me. Digging, scraping, and leaving me raw and desperate.

"Hey, you ok?" Alanna asks as I slide down the wall. My mind seems trapped in the past, and trapped in that hell hole.

"Fuck, woman down!" Someone screams as my eyes blink. The view goes from white cabinets to black and then silver.

Chapter 19

Maria

One Year and Ten Months Ago.

I had tried. That's all I could've done, I tell myself as I walk out of the clubhouse. The guy told me there was no one here named Crow. Although, he was giving me the creeps.

He had this look about himself that had my stomach twist in on its self.

"Need some help?" His voice came from behind me. I whirled around and stumbled at the fast movement. Dizziness was keeping me unsteady.

"No," I tell him, begging the world to be still.

His smile got even more creepy, and my heart lodged into my throat. What was he even doing here? Did he follow me? Looking down at my flat tire, I sigh. I was in the process of changing it when he had appeared out of what feels like nowhere.

"Seriously, I'm good," I tell him. I shouldn't have turned my back on him! What was I thinking? His hand latched onto my hair, yanking me into his body.

"No, baby, but you will be," he whispered into my hair.

I shuddered in revulsion and tried to twist away from him. When his arm tightened around my waist, and his fingers tugged my hair hard, I cried out.

Panic started to set in. I couldn't let this happen to me. He kept my head immobile, so I couldn't headbutt him. Lifting my foot, I slammed it down on his foot before lifting it and kicking him in the left shin as hard as I could.

He still didn't let me go, but his arm did leave my waist. Yes! I pulled my head and let the tears fall as a strand of hair was ripped from my head. It was better than the alternative, I told myself.

"Fucking bitch," he whispered coldly into my ear, "I'm going to fucking love tearing you up."

My heart stopped at his words. Oh, god, no, no, no, no. I wasn't going to be a statistic.

"Someone wants you, but I think we'll have a little fun first," he tells me, his voice husky.

"No," I whispered. The words were hard to get out.

"Raoul is looking for you," he tells me.

"As much as I want to take you right fucking here, baby. We don't have time. But after he's done with you, that pussy is mine," he tells me as he grinds his hard jean cover dick into my ass.

A cloth was pressed over my nose and mouth, and I held my breath as long as I could, but it was no use. My body needed oxygen, and it refused to let me suffocate. But darkness soon swallowed me.

Hell was where I ended up, a place I never thought existed. I learned exactly where it was and how real it was.

Someone shaking me and they were screaming my name. I look up and see Crow and start screaming again.

"Don't touch me," my lungs burn as the words blast from my lips.

Lincoln is standing behind Crow staring down at me, his eyes are cold. It is him, the man who told me Crow wasn't a member. The man who stole my innocence, my life, and my freedom. The very man who dragged me to hell.

"Maria, baby, please," Crow begs.

I want to respond, I want to beg him to save me, but I am pulled in, and I can't get out.

One Year and Nine Months Ago.

The metal chained to my foot rattled as I shifted on the floor. It was so hot in here, I tried to press myself further onto the concrete floor. I was hoping it would cool my overheated body.

I could hear the music and laughter coming from inside the building. I was in the garage where I've been for the last thirty days.

I haven't seen the sun for a long time, and I have tried to keep track of time from the smell of the food they cook. Who knows, maybe it's been longer?

My back burned as my sweat dripped onto my scabs and freshly made cuts. Raoul liked to make small one-inch cuts on my body.

The cuts were on my breasts, upper stomach, and the middle of my back. They were always in places that could be covered up. The first night here was the worst.

The way his fingers ran up my thigh made me feel like bugs were crawling all over my skin. I closed my eyes as the feeling of him covering me overrode the pain in my abused body.

When he ripped my panties off, I begged him to not do what he was about to do. I even told him about the baby. I thought he would ignore me as I begged him in desperation, but instead, he pulled back. He then grabbed a fistful of my hair forcing my head to turn at an odd angle.

"You're pregnant?" he spits.

I didn't figure Raoul was a man of morals and it seemed he was only with this. When I nodded, I watched him through blurry eyes. He growled and released me, shoving my head down.

"Fuck! You lucky bitch," he snarled.

I heard a few mummers of disappointment. How many men were in here?

"You said we would get some of that pussy," one man growled.

I then heard silence, the only thing that could be heard was my quiet sobs. I screamed when I heard the bang and a body collapsing to the floor.

"Anyone else got something to fucking say?" Raoul demanded.

A few feet shifted, but not a word was said.

"Now, I may not fuck her pussy, at least not yet, but I can mark her pretty little body," his voice had this odd sound, almost like it was filled with glee.

The pain sliced into me, and my heated blood welled as I felt the sharp metal press into me, repeatedly. It slowly slid through layers of skin and tissue.

At some point I passed out, thankful for the reprieve. Laughter rang in my ears as they watched Raoul mark my body over and over.

Chapter 20

Maria

Present Day.

Hands are running through my hair as a hard body is pressed against me.

"I've got you," Crow is whispering over and over again.

"Oh, Maria," Ronnie cries as she pushes Crow with her knee.

"My cheeks are wet and warm. People are staring at me. Lincoln is still close, closer than I ever want him to be.

His feet are maybe a foot from my elbow. My eyes look up into his, and I try to climb over Crow's shoulder. I need to get away.

I didn't recognize Lincoln when I first got here. I didn't really connect him to what happened. Now I remember, and Lincoln was definitely the one who captured me. He also took me to Raoul, and I need to get away from him. Now!

"Maria, stop," Crow snaps.

"NO! Get away from me! Oh, god, stay away from me," I cry as I continue to fight Crow. Lincoln is too close.

"Save Shawn, Ronnie," I shout to her.

"Maria?" Ronnie asks, her voice is filled with concern and has tears in her eyes.

"He's here. He's going to take me back! Save Shawn. Run, oh god, run," I scream again, pleading with her as I try to get away.

Crow's arms tighten further on my waist, and he pulls me back onto his lap. I shy away from Lincoln who is pressing further into Crow's chest.

"Fuck!" Ronnie whispers as she scans the surrounding faces.

"You promised," I remind her, "Take him and go." My throat is raw and cracking as I try to get Ronnie to move.

"She takes a step back while holding Shawn, who is crying into her chest. Ronnie is looking at all the men filling the room. A few were at her back blocking the exit to the kitchen.

She ran into one and squeaked. Her eyes are hardening as she turns and tries to push the man out of the way.

"I won't tell, please don't hurt him," I cry harder.

I knew Lincoln could hear me, but I was too terrified to look at him. There was no safe place for us. No one could save me now.

"Get the fuck out now!" Crow shouts at everyone. I watch as they start to move to the door.

"NO! Ronnie, please stay. Don't go, please, it's not safe," I tell her once again, trying to escape Crow.

"Stay the fuck still!" Crow growls in my ear,

"Don't go out there," I tell Ronnie. She nods and watches each member as they leave the kitchen. It's as if there are venomous snakes. Just ready to attack at any moment.

"What the fuck is going on Maria?" Crow demands.

I can't look him in the eye. There is too much to read there. He would see, and he would know I wasn't human anymore. I was dirt and very scared.

"Ronnie," I whisper, brokenly.

"I've got him," she tells me quietly.

"Take my son to your room," Crow tells Ronnie.

"NO! Don't go out there, you can't go out there," I scream again.

"What the fuck, Maria!" Crow snaps, having reached the end of his patience, "Tell me what the fuck is going on. Right, the fuck now."

"HE's out there," I whisper, brokenly.

"Are you sure?" Ronnie asks me, her voice gentle and comforting.

"Yes, it's him," I look up at Ronnie.

"Who the fuck is 'him'?" Crow growls.

My hands become the most interesting things in the world. My eyes are now glued to them.

"I can't tell you," I whisper.

"The fuck you can't," Crow snaps.

"Maria," Ronnie whispers.

"No, don't you dare," I tell her coldly.

"We can't leave, you know that," she reminds me of what is out there waiting for us.

"I didn't just leave here two years ago," I take a deep breath. This isn't going to be easy.

Ronnie sits down on my right and grabs my hands. I am still sitting in Crows lap.

"IS there anyone you can trust with Shawn?" Ronnie asks.

"NO!" I cry.

"One of the old ladies?" Crow asks her.

I shudder as both fear and heartbreak rock my body.

"The girls that were just in here?" Ronnie asks Crow.

"Yes," he tells her before calling out to Alanna.

"Only them, no one else. No one else can be with Shawn, and I want to be able to see him," I demand.

I may be a mess, but I am not letting that man near my son.

"Shawn can't be here for this, Maria," Ronnie tells me gently.

My head lowers, I know she's right. I had been a screaming mess, and I know that he is already terrified. His little arms are wrapped tightly around Ronnie's neck.

The girls from before appeared. Looking into the room all of them concerned.

"Get Reyes and Gunner and go sit in my office," Crow demands.

I look at them before looking up at Crow.

"I want to see Reyes and Gunner before you let them take our son," I command.

I watch as two men fill the doorway, I recognize neither of them.

"Could have brought the kids," the darker haired one said.

I start to relax a little and nod to Ronnie. "Stay with them," I tell her.

"You don't need me here?" she asks.

"No, watch Shawn," I tell her.

She nods and stands, following the group out of the room and closes the door behind her. My chest heaves as the walls start to close on me. I feel like I am going back there, into the nightmares.

"What the fuck is going on Maria?" Crow asks, his tone harsh.

"Why do you care?" I ask him.

"Please?" he begs.

"I came here looking for you, and one of the members told me there was no one here called Crow. His smile made me sick, nervous, and extremely uncomfortable."

Looking at my hands, I tug on my fingers trying to keep myself grounded.

"I thought it was over when I left, that I would never see you again," I give Crow a humorous laugh, trying to continue the story. "I got a flat tire three miles down the road and poof he was there."

I swallow. My voice is lowering as Lincoln's dark desire-filled eyes fill my mind.

"He grabbed me and made all kinds of promises, promises I knew he was going to follow through with. But someone else wanted me first," I croak.

They are coming for me in my nightmares. The ones that stalk me while I sleep and while I am awake.

"He took me to hell, a place where nightmares begin and never end," I swallow, my throat is raw, and tears fill my eyes.

I was back there living and watching as if I am a voyeur. For the first time, I am not reliving them completely, just watching them on the sidelines. I keep talking and continue to tell Crow everything.

"It was always so dark unless he came to play. The heat was unbearable, and the stench of pennies and motor oil filled the air.

There was this heavy chain on my ankle, and it was rusty and wet. It would scrap my skin with my every move. My raw skin became sensitive and stung.

My clothes were torn from the first day, and it was all I had left. I had this long soft skirt that fell to my knees, at least it did before he took a knife to it. Said it needed some trimming, easier access."

Crow's arms tighten around me as growls leave his throat. He is also shaking.

"He took my panties and shirt the very first day. I thought that would be the worse than anything else that could possibly be done to me. Oh, god, was I wrong?

I still feel the cold metal as it was pressed harder and harder into my skin, parting the flesh slowly. It was right on my spine, and I thought, god, he's going to go all the way down to the bone.

The scent of pennies grew stronger as my screams mixed with their laughter. I finally understood why the garage had the smell of pennies.

When he finally pulled the blade back, I lowered myself further to the floor. I was hoping for relief, hoping he was finished. But he was so angry that I was pregnant. Who knew a monster like him had morals.

He hated that he couldn't rape me. Some of the men weren't too happy about it either. I remember the sound of a body hitting the floor after one of them made their displeasure known.

The days blended together. I counted them by judging the food that was being cooked. I thought I had only been there thirty days, but I had lost time passing out from blood loss and pain.

One of them wanted their turn with me and decided not to listen to the orders. The guy came and unchained my ankles. He shoved a rag into my mouth and dragged me out into the night.

I remembered looking up the stars as he pulled me by my arms through the grass. I was so tired, and everything hurt. At this point, there was a small bump in my lower stomach. Shawn had still been growing, even though I was surviving in less than ideal circumstances.

I told myself I wasn't going to let them take any more from me. I wasn't going to let him do this to me. I waited as he climbed on me and focused on his belt.

I lifted both my hands and pressed my fingers into his eyes, hard. He fell back with a scream. The gag I had in my mouth was quickly out and went into his.

His gun was lying next to my hip. I didn't know how cold the metal was or how heavy it would be until that moment. It was like I checked out. This cold detachment came over me as I pulled the trigger and watched his head explode. Literally, explode. He collapsed on my legs.

I knew I didn't have much time. They were going to be coming. Twisting out from under him, I bit back the screams of pain as my scabs were ripped open.

I'm not sure what happened after that, I remember running. Ronnie told me she found me in her backyard four months after I left here. She took me in, and she saved me," I finished hoarsely.

Crow is just looking down on me. I need to feel his love even if he hates me, I need to feel him inside of me to chase away the memories. It is irrational and fucked up, I know that.

But I needed to feel something other than fear and disgust. This man was once my world, the only person to make me feel loved.

His eyes are dark green orbs and filled with anger and something else that I can't put my finger on. Closing my eyes, I take a deep breath and rip at the button of his jeans and his zipper.

Stradling his hips, I tug my underwear aside and sink down on his hard, thick cock. I lift myself up and down over and over until he is finally all the way inside of me.

I moan into his shoulder as I fuck him hard. I continue to lift myself up and dropping myself back down over and over, swiveling my hips and pressing my clit into his pelvic bone.

It didn't take long before we were both moaning our release. I felt Crow's cum jet into me in hard pulses sending little shudders of pleasure through me.

"Fuck, doll," he whispers into my hair.

Maybe I did it so I didn't have to see his pity. Maybe because I need to feel alive and forget the past. Or it was because I still love him, god help me, but I do still love him.

"Who took you?" Crow whispers into my hair pressing a comforting kiss to my head.

His cock was still deep inside me and hard as a rock.

"Lincoln," I tell him pressing my face into his neck and taking deep breaths. Filling my lungs with his scent. Chasing away the fear that gripped me as his name left my lips.

His arms tighten around me. I could feel the moment he went from lover to killer. I knew what was about to happen and something in me cheered, bringing a smile to my lips.

"I want you in my room and my bed," he tells me.

"I can't do that, we can't do this, Crow," I tell him sadly.

There is too much shit between us. Fuck, he hates me. Why would he want this? Was it as sick punishment?

"We had a deal, I'm calling in my marker. You're mine. Period," he growls.

His hands pull me closer to him and his cock jerks deep inside of me. Oh god, that feels so good. His hand tunnels through my hair, fisting it tightly. He pulls my head until I am looking up at him.

"I'm going to fucking kill every last one of them, doll. I can promise you that," he tells me, looking deep into my eyes before pressing a punishing kiss to my lips.

"Reyes and his brothers will help you move and guard you until I get back," he tells me as he lifts me from his lap.

I feel our combined juices slide down my thighs. My panties are still not in place.

"Fuck, that is the sexiest thing I've ever seen," my cheeks heat.

He may want me now, but he hasn't seen me without my clothes on. I am not the girl he remembers. It is something I need to remind myself. Because when he does discard me, I want to be prepared for the pain that is going to come with it.

Chapter 21

Crow

Present Day.

Cupping her face, I kiss her forehead before stepping away from her. Her eyes are filled with darkness and distrust.

I thought she fucking left me and had this poster life. Another man and maybe the perfect little house in a perfect little neighborhood. Not once did I fucking think she was living the shit she did.

Red coated my vision as anger road me hard. I was going to fucking kill him. Lincoln was a dead man. After everything she told me, I was ready to rip him limb from limb.

I need answers. Looking over at Gage and Weston, I tilt my head showing them we need to talk before I call church.

I am going to find out who was there, and I am going to hunt every motherfucker and kill them slowly. My fist tightens even more, and my short nails dig into the calluses on the palms of my hand.

"What the fuck was that shit?" Gage demands.

I turn and look at them. They both look ready to destroy everything in sight. That shit was painful to fucking watch let alone hear the story behind it.

"Someone took her when she left here," I tell them, my eyes hard.

"Fuck!" Weston growls.

"What the fuck happened to her?" Gage asks, his tone dark.

"Fucking Lincoln took her to someone who kept her fucking chained and carved her up like a fucking piece of meat," I snarl, my hands slam onto the office desk. The wood split and some of the contents tumble off.

"What are we going to do?" Gage gets right to it.

"Call Church in ten, but I want you to let Knox know what the fuck is going on," I tell them both.

I watch as they turn to go, but before Weston leaves, he asks something. It was something I was thinking just a few minutes ago.

"Are you keeping her?"

I look him in the eye trying to see if he has a thing for her. Finding nothing but curiosity, I sit in my chair running my hands through my hair.

"Fuck man, I'm never letting her go," I tell him honestly.

"Good," he replies as the door closes behind him.

I want to rip this place apart. My anger and grief are riding me hard. Maria may have left, but it was not of her own will. If I only looked harder.

I walk into the room and purposely look around making sure Lincoln was still in the main room. The fucking piece of shit is sitting at the bar drinking a beer like he didn't have a care in the world.

"Church, now," I shout.

Chairs scrap back as they all fill into the other room. I wait for Lincoln to try and run or come up with some fucking reason why he can't be in there.

He actually swaggers into the god damn room like he is holding the key to the fucking kingdom. Does he really think she will keep his secret?

Walking to my chair at the head of the table, I look to my right and see Gage nod, letting me know he informed Knox.

Weston sits to my left looking like he is bored as fuck. But I know the truth, he wants to kill the bastard just as much as I do.

"We have a little problem. Someone took my old lady and carved her up like a fucking turkey at Thanksgiving," I tell them, my eyes scan all their faces.

Who could I trust? Was any of them in on it? Everyone's face turned cold but Lincoln. The anger and darkness that lurks deep within us all is starting to come to my surface.

"We have a fucking traitor," Gage announces.

Another look at the faces of each man in this room. None show any signs of betrayal. All but Lincoln, who just sits there.

"Do we have any idea who it is?" Zeke asks darkly.

Nodding to Gage and Weston, I watch as they circle the table heading towards Lincoln. Gage circles from the right and Weston from the left.

Gage pulls his gun and presses it against Lincoln's head as Weston leans in close.

"We are going to have so much fucking fun," he tells Lincoln gleefully.

"Seems Lincoln told Maria I wasn't a member and then took her," I tell the other brothers. They all look at Lincoln in disgust.

"Take him to the basement," I tell them.

I watch as they drag a pleading Lincoln from the room. Screaming that the bitch is a liar.

"I want you to be ready. I'm going to find out who every motherfucker is and then we're going to hunt each and every one of them down," I tell them as I scan the room. I meet everyone's eyes.

I got nods before they pull back from the table and leave the room. Running my hands over my head, I sigh. Reign your shit in, you can't fucking kill him too soon. I had to remind myself of that each time I punched him, cut him, and put the drill to his knees. I relished every scream, and he gave them up so fast hoping I would just kill him.

The dumb fuck had no idea. I was going to drag this out for a long, long fucking time.

Chapter 22

Maria

Present Day.

I've been sitting on the bed for what feels like hours. Crow came in covered in blood. I knew exactly whose blood it was and felt nothing but relief and a small amount of joy.

Ronnie took Shawn to get lunch and ice cream that Gage promised him. I smiled when the big man hovered over Ronnie. He had no idea what he was in for.

The water finally shuts off, and my nerves kicked into high gear. What is Crow going to do? He wants me here and has told me that I am his. That can mean so many things, right?

I suck in a deep breath as Crow comes out wearing a white towel around his waist. Water droplets slide over his skin and disappear into the towel.

I lick my lips fighting the urge to follow those drops with my tongue. Is it wrong to be jealous of the water on Crow's skin?

"Crow?" I whisper as he stands there with one hand on the towel. The other is at the top of the dresser, and he isn't moving. Nothing but deep breaths can be heard.

I watch as he turns to me. The look of hunger in Crow's eyes makes my clit throb. Were we really going to do this, again?

I scoot up the bed as he closes the distance between us. Hunger and desire are written all over his face.

"I fucking need you," he growls.

My pussy clenches and unclenches at his words. Heat fills my face and need almost overwhelms me. My hands pull my shirt over my head, and I quickly undo my bra.

My eyes slam shut as I remember what I look like. The marks are all over my ribs and boobs. Quickly, my hands raise up to cover myself.

"No, let me see," he demands.

My eyes close even tighter, refusing to open and see his face as he takes in the damage to my body. The bed dips under his weight, and I know he is closing the gap between us.

I gasp as a rough finger presses against one of the more raised scars. I shudder.

"So, fucking beautiful," he whispers, his breath fans over my exposed breast. I feel his lips press against the scar and then the next and so on. Each time he mutters how beautiful I am.

My heart melts under both his words and kisses. Wetness coats my thighs, having taken my panties off earlier. They were too wet and extremely uncomfortable.

"Please, I need you," I tell him, my eyes remain closed.

"Look at me darlin'," he commands. "Are you on any birth control?"

My eyes open, and I focus on him. Slowly, I shake my head. My eyes lower again as I watch him pull off the towel. He settles quickly between my parted thighs. His hands grip my hips, pushing my skirt up around my waist. Then, he presses himself deep inside of me in one long, hard thrust.

I moan when he is fully seated, and his cock hits my womb. My head falls back and my back arches, bringing my chest closer to his.

"Someday I'm going to fucking get you completely naked before I fuck this pretty pussy," he growls as he slams into me again and again.

"Oh, god," I moan.

"I'm also going to eat this sweet pussy, too," he tells me as he pumps his hips into me hard. His words cause wetness to gush between my thighs.

"Fuck, darlin' you're so goddamn tight," he moans.

Another long stroke has my nails rake his back. It seems to fuel him on because as soon as my nails sink into his hard-muscular shoulder, he slams into me harder.

Drilling me into the bed, harder and harder. My throat is raw from screaming as Crow picks up the pace.

"I'm going to fill this pussy full of my cum, baby," he groans.

My answering moan is breathless as my toes curl, and I hurtle over the edge. Every muscle is locking up in my body.

"That's right, cum on my cock," he growls and pumps into me a few more times. Then heat fills me so much I am not sure I could contain it.

"I can get pregnant," I whisper against this neck.

"Then I'll be doing my fucking job," he tells me and presses a kiss to my lips.

His dick is still deep inside of me as he rolls over, taking me with him. I go to move, but he latches onto me.

"Don't," he demands.

Lowering myself back down, I let my face rest on his chest. Soon exhaustion swallows me.

My last thought before I let the world fade completely is what the fuck had I just done?

Chapter 22

Maria

Three Weeks Later.

Crow has been gone more than he's been home. Every time he comes back covered in blood, he would go right to the shower. He'd stay in there for what felt like an eternity.

I know what he is doing, and a part of me is relieved. Like this deep fear is slowly lifting. How many are left?

I watch as he comes out of the bathroom with a towel wrapped around his waist. His eyes go to the crib which holds our son and then to me.

"It's over," he tells me, pulling me in close.

"Over?" I ask that could mean so many things.

"Every one of those fuckers is dead," he whispers into my hair.

I sag into him, and relief fills me. Only for tension to fill me again. There is still the Albanians.

"What about the Albanians?" I whisper into his chest.

"We'll figure that shit out too, doll," he tells me before pulling my head back, so I am looking up at him. Those sinful lips press against mine and devour me.

"You taste so fuckin good," he growls.

Putting my hands on his chest, I gently push him in the direction of the bed. I know he only budges because he wants to.

Once he is seated, I lift the purple silk nightgown over my head. My hands shake as I part the towel, my desire for him is so strong. I am shaking with need.

"Fuck, darlin' let me taste you," he growls, trying to eat my pussy. Later, I need him inside of me, now.

Throwing one leg over his waist, I straddle him with one knee on either side of his hips. Gripping his huge cock, I line it up with my entrance and drop down taking it, one inch at a time.

When I feel him hit my womb, I start to bounce in his lap moaning as his lips wrap around my nipple sucking it into his mouth.

"Oh, god," I moan quietly.

"So, fucking wet for me," he whispers against my wet beaded nipple.

"I'm pregnant," I tell him as I fuck him harder.

He groans as I take him in deeper, my words not registering. As I fall over the edge, he thrusts up into me. His hand holds the back of my neck as he stands and turns us. Now my back is pressed to the bed.

Then he is really fucking me. The bed shakes, and I would have slid, had he not been holding me in place. His groans mix with my moans, and I race towards another orgasm.

I feel him jerk deep inside of me and know he is close. I press my lips to his ear and whisper the words I know will have him explode.

"I'm pregnant," I bite.

"Fuck," he groans as he empties himself inside of me. His hand tightened on my neck as he shoves his oversized cock as deep as it will go.

When he is finished, he lifts me from the bed and carries me to the top. All while he is lodged deep inside of me. Little moans escape with each step he takes.

My eyes closed as exhaustion swamps me. I feel the bed shift as Crow slides in behind me. His arms pull me close to him.

"Are you sure?" He asks as his hand cups my flat stomach.

"Yes," I smile.

"I fucking love you," he whispers into my ear as his fingers move gently over my tummy where our child is growing.

"I love you too," I tell him.

Find out what happens with the Albanians and what Ronnie is running from in Destroying Gage coming soon.

Follow Me

Facebook- http://ow.ly/mMVp30jtWMx
Twitter- Twitter.com/@RoxanneGreening
My Amazon page- http://ow.ly/a9o930jtX6n
Www.authorroxannegreening.wordpress.com
Goodreads- http://ow.ly/vR9K30cBq8R
Instagram.com/authorroxannegreening
BookBub- http://ow.ly/JXVH30jtWFx

Other Ways To Contact Me:

Authorroxannegreening@yahoo.com

Author Roxanne Greening

P.O. Box 624

Parkersburg, W.V. 26101

Keep Going For A Sneak Peek At Some Of My Other Books!

Mia's Wolf

BlackRoads Pack Book 1

Prologue:

I couldn't believe my eyes, Jack was running his fingers over Sally's thigh. I continue to watch as he comes closer to the hem of her short skirt. That bastard! He's a cheating, no good, low-down scum of the earth.

There was no mistaking the pair. The sun shimmered off their hair. Jack's overly blond and Sally's bleach bottle blond hair could not be missed. He was basically fucking her under the tree which was near the picnic table that I normal ate my lunch at.

Today I had planned to go to the Halloween store to find a costume for tomorrow night's party. But at the last minute, I decided to eat my lunch at my favorite spot. Well, it's not my favorite anymore.

Currently, I was standing over Jack and Sally and watched their progress. Jack had the top down on his luxurious convertible, so I could see them clearly. My hand started to clench the cold soft drink that I was holding. The condensation on the sides became slippery against my fingers. Then, a wicked smile started to blossom over my face.

I loved the south, even in October. It was still warm, but it had a small bite of cool air. As I stood there, I reminded myself that Jack thought I was shopping. Oh, how wrong he was!

His hand slid a little farther up Sally's barely there fabric, and my teeth sank into my lip as my hand clenched my cup a little harder.

"Oh, Jack," Sally whispered in a husky voice, and my stomach revolted at the sound.

"That's it, babe," Jack tells Sally as his non-calloused fingers climbed higher up the inside of her thigh.

The bile that I was fighting rose a little higher.

"Oh, Jack," I mimicked Sally when she said his name in a breathless husky tone.

I mean really? What the fuck! Sally couldn't find her own boyfriend, why did she have to go fuck mine?

Satisfaction hit me like a runaway train as both froze in place. Jack quickly moved his hand and straightened up in his seat. He tried to look innocent and obviously he failed.

I should be crying, right? Maybe even shed some tears. Instead, I felt nothing but anger and regret? I didn't regret not sleeping with him, so why did I feel this deep regret?

"Mia, it's not what it looks like, babe," he tells me.

His voice grated on my nerves, I mean, do I look blind? Was I some sort of airhead? I could see exactly what was happening here.

"So, you didn't come to my favorite spot and feel Sally up?" I ask in a sickly-sweet voice.

"Mia," Sally says, her voice filled with a slight chill like the cool air of October.

"Bitch," I tell her.

Her eyes grew bigger, and her mouth turned down into a frown. Although, I had a big smile that was all teeth.

"Look, Mia…" Jack started.

The hand that was holding my drink continued to squeeze. The longer I stood there, the tighter my hand squeezed the cup. My fingers twitched when Jack said my name, and it caused the top to pop off. The plastic cup splashed everywhere, and Sally was the unfortunate victim of the soda. It poured all over her, and my toothy smile grew.

"I'm sorry, babe," I snarled, "But it seems we have hit a rough patch in the road."

"Mia," he tried again, but his voice sounded desperate.

"I think this is where our trip together ends, Jack," I tell him with fake sincerity.

I leaned in closer, and the half-empty cup was still clutched in my hand. Sally leaned back to give me room, but she was probably fearful that I might bite her. Who the hell knows, maybe I will.

"I wouldn't spread my fucking thighs for you, so you go to Sally?" I ask him, "And what makes you think that you could fuck her and then come back to me?"

I don't wait for a response, I just release the cup that I was holding and followed its decent with my eyes. It was like watching a car wreck in slow motion. It was falling, and then it hit Jack's lap with a thud. The rest of the cola sprayed all over his lap. I'm sure it hurt his little balls, the impact was pretty hard.

"I'm going to the party without you, Jack," I tell him coldly.

He could probably feel his status already starting to drop. He wasn't invited to the party in the woods, I was. And well, my plus one just went to minus one.

"Mia, please," Jack calls after me as I speed walk away from the pair. My forgotten lunch still dangling from my fingers.

Being a senior in college was hard. This was our last hurrah before we walked across the stage. I thought I was going to marry Jack Dalton and become Mrs. Mia Dalton. Fucking asshole. After today, he would be just a smudge on my past, and I wouldn't remember who and what he was to me.

Chapter 1

Bastien

There was a rouge on our property. It kept toeing the line, and as alpha, it was my job to see the fucker off Blackroad's property.

I walked through the pack's land watching as the children played and the autumn leaves fall to the hard ground. Autumn was my favorite time of the year. The various scents that were released as the cold started to set in was my favorite.

Before Dirk said a word, I smelled him. He smelled like moss and fresh grass.

"Bastien," Dirk shouted.

Turning I looked at the pack enforcer. He was jogging away from the cabins.

"Yeah?" I asked him.

"The fucker's scent was picked up in the west," he tells me.

"Did anyone see him?" I growled. This rouge wolf had a way of just coming a few minutes before a sentinel was passing by. He was lucky, a little too lucky for my taste.

"No," Dirk said while he shook his head and clenched his fist.

This bastard was toying with us. We were chasing our own fucking tails.

"Alpha," a little hand tugged on my black t-shirt. Turning, I look down at Tommy.

"Tommy," I acknowledged him with a smile. I couldn't keep the smile off my face.

"Look what I found," he said while he held up his little hand proudly. I crouched down and examined the little stones that he held in his fist like they were national treasures.

"You found some pretty amazing rocks," I tell him as a calm started to settle over me. He didn't need to feel the anger and frustration I felt.

His little five-year-old chest puffed up with pride. He was going to be a great sentinel when he got older. I could see it in the way he presented himself.

"You should go show your mom what you found. I bet she's going to love them," I tell him gently.

His eyes grew round as he turned from me. His little legs took him as fast as he could go in search of his mother.

"Call in my beta and a few of the sentinels. We need to have a meeting," I sighed as I stood up. This fucker needed to be brought down before someone got hurt.

Chapter 2

Mia

Stella: I can't believe Jack would do something like that.

I reread Stella's text and sighed.

Me: I should have seen it coming.

Stella: Bitch, please! Four fucking years with that dick. I didn't see it coming, and I wasn't even with him.

I laughed hard as I read what she wrote.

Me: He thought I was fucking stupid. 'Mia, it's not what it looks like.' Yeah, your hand wasn't just almost in her snatch.

Stella: Wish I could have seen his face.

Me: He looked like a dying fish.

Stella: Oh, god, and I missed it!

My phone shook as I remembered his face. Laughter bubbled up.

Stella: Going solo?

Me: Fuck, my plus one was doing his own plus one.

Stella: In a place where so many have gone before….

Me: Why does that remind me of Star Trek, the old tv show?

Stella: Because you are full of awesomeness.

Me: I know ☐

Stella: What are you going to be?

I looked down at my Little Red Riding Hood costume. The red cape was long and silky. I pulled up my short jean shorts and adjusted my tight red top. It showed just a hint of my stomach.

My army boots would make stomping through the forest a little less of a hazard for my feet. Basically, I was Little Red on steroids. The thought made me smile.

Me: Little Red Riding Hood.

Stella: Boring…

Me: Little Red on steroids.

Stella: On the sexy side, I hope.

Me: No shit!

Me: What about you?

Stella: What about me?

Me: What are you going as?

Stella: Jane

Me: Jane?

Stella: Hoping for my Tarzan ☐

Me: Ugh! Jack won't leave me alone! ☹

Jack kept calling me, and I was at the point where I considered blocking his number. Didn't he get the fucking hint yesterday? If not, he should have when I never answered the hundred and twenty times he called since then. I wish I were exaggerating on how many times he called!

I never gave him the location of the party, I figured we were going together, and it wouldn't matter. At least not until it was time to head in that direction.

Anger coursed through my veins at the thought of Jack. I waisted four fucking years on that bastard. Two in high school and two here in college.

I love kids, so I decided to take an early childhood development class. I loved it and decided to get a degree in it. It was something he didn't understand and didn't support. That right there should have sent up a red flag.

The thought of working with children in a few weeks brought a smile to my face. Their little hands and sweet faces were always excited over the simplest of things.

Stella: Tell him to fuck off!

Me: God, I hate this shit.

Could it get any worse? Then I remembered, I needed to go to our apartment and clear out my shit. Jack and I moved in together two years into our relationship. Neither of us wanted to live in the dorms.

He hated, and I guess pretended to respect, my no sex until marriage rule. Looking back, I think I just didn't want him to be my first.

Stella: You're a hot babe. You'll find someone, and Jack will be the man you never remember. Maybe you'll get lucky and find someone tonight.

Me: Yeah sure, Mr. Right is just going to come waltzing along and save me from the big bad wolf.

Stella: One can dream, babe! Maybe we'll find us a set of brothers….

Me: You are so bad!

Stella: That's why you love me. ☐

I laughed. She's right, that's why I love her. She makes me laugh, and she's always there for me. She's more adventurous then I could ever be.

Sighing I sat heavily in the chair. The hotel room was clean, quiet and empty. I missed having someone holding me close as I slept. The warmth of Jacks body always kept the cold away.

Bending over, I tied my boots while berating myself for such thoughts. *You hate Jack, remember? He's been fucking Sally and who knows how many others! Probably been doing it your whole relationship.*

How I wish that voice was wrong, but I was positive it was right. You are not going back, it screamed.

Like fucking hell, I was! I scream back.

Whatever Jack and I had was over, and it didn't hurt, not even a little. These moments of sorrow were phantom memories. A comfortable routine that is set off course. Like a train that derailed.

Jack: Please, Mia.

Me: Fuck off, Jack!

Jack: It didn't mean anything, babe.

Me: Stop. Fucking. Calling. Me.

Jack: I love you…

Me: I don't love you, Jack, leave me alone, please!

Jack: Don't do this.

Me: I will block you!

Jack: Mia, babe, it was one fucking mistake. You're really going to throw away four years?

Me: At least you do not deny it.

Jack: Come on babe. You're really going to throw away four years over one mistake?

Me: Those four years are like a smudge in my life. A little blurry and already forgotten.

Me: Just once? Your hand looked awfully comfortable climbing its way towards her snatch.

Jack: Mia, come on, let's move past this.

Me: Already done that. Goodbye Jack.

After I sent the last message, I waited with suspended breath for him to try again and was blissfully relieved when my phone didn't make a peep. Maybe he finally got it through his head. It was over the minute he touched her.

It was over long before that, the damn voice reminded me.

Oh, stuff a sock in it! I told it.

Standing, I slipped a few twenties into my back pocket with my driver's license and room key. I wasn't taking a purse tonight since I knew I was going to party hard. I deserved a good night of forgotten bullshit and alcohol-induced fun.

**Craving Zane
Grimm Brothers MC
Book 4**

Prologue:
Two Years Ago.

I remember the day he walked in, and I tried to save him. If I knew then it was going to turn into a shit storm, I would have locked the door before he could walk through it.

It was just before closing when he sauntered in. My eyes met his over the table I was cleaning. His dark gray T-shirt clung to him perfectly. It stretched over a beautifully muscular chest. His thick toned legs were encased in dark blue jeans that wrapped around his lower half deliciously.

There was an instant throb between my legs. A need deep in the pit of my stomach. A horrible clawing ache in my chest. It left a horrible taste in my mouth. Fear. There was something about him, as cliché as that sounds, he looked like someone who needed to be saved. Not just in the bad boy needs a good woman kind of way.

Color me stupid, but I didn't want to see him end up like a few others. Those poor fucks. No one deserved to die like that. It was horrifying to watch as the person's legs and arms were grabbed and swung back and forth like a hammock blowing in the wind before being tossed from the boat. At least it was a big boat that they got to cruise in, it was luxury for their small amount of time. Hello, bright side. That is before being dropped into international waters with some hungry sharks. The blood poured from the body which caused the sharks into a feeding frenzy.

I cringed at the memory. I had been forced to attend the gruesome burial. I was property, and the club wanted me to keep the drinks flowing.

Shaking away the memory, I became more thankful then I've been in years. The others had gravitated to the back of the bar, leaving me alone out here.

Clutching the rag, I all but tripped over myself trying to reach him before he got too far into the bar and unlucky enough to be seen by one of the bikers.

"Listen to me you need to get out of here," I begged him. My eyes pleading.

His eyes narrowed, but he said nothing. His eyes seemed to question, why the fuck should I do that?

"This is a biker bar. These guys will literally kill you if you're not careful," I tell him slowly. Hoping the words would sink in deep. I can't help but to glance over my shoulder hoping they stayed back there.

Again, he says nothing just raised an eyebrow. A silent challenge.

That night changed everything. It was the beginning of the end.

Chapter 1
Tori
Earlier That Night...

If you asked me two years, three months, and forty-six days ago if I would be at this bar wiping tables and dodging roaming hands, I would have laughed in your face and called it a sick joke. But that's not the case.

I'm here in this stinky, filthy bar listening to the sounds of my feet sticking to the nasty floor, the laughs of the sweaty bikers who view me as nothing more than pussy on legs, and the hum of the piece of shit air conditioner.

I leaned over the wooden table surface and set another beer down. These fuckers liked to make me work for it. Not once have they held up a hand or reached for their beers. My short legs stretched to their limits, and my toes strained as I reached as far as I could.

Just as my fingers released the cold, wet bottle of beer, a hand slid up the back of my thigh. The calloused hand felt rough against my bare leg. It was like sandpaper against my skin. I fought the cringe that tried to appear on my face. Instead, I plastered a smile and rocked back onto my heels.

Sidestepping his roaming hands, I once again cursed the dress code (I snort if you could call it that) the bar owner forced us ladies to wear. I had to wear short shorts, and they were so short my ass cheeks spilled out, and a too-small tank top that was completely stretched to its limits over my breasts that they almost pop out.

"Tori," Jack called from the bar.

Relief had me almost sagging.

"Enjoy your drinks boys," I tell them with my fake megawatt smile.

The club owned me. I feared the day they decided I was club girl material. I wasn't so sure I could fight them off. My father, the bastard, borrowed enough money to keep me in their employment for the next five years. Then he bounced not caring that he was leaving me behind to pay for his mistakes.

"Tori," Deke smirked. He was the president of the club, and also known as the man trying to cop a feel a few moments ago.

I turned to look at him. My silence was a safety measure, it was something I learned that quickly kept me alive and pain-free.

Rule number one, don't question them. Period. Rule number two, woman were to spread their legs whenever and wherever the club members chose or get the fuck out. Unless, of course, they own you. Then you get a small safety feature. I'm honestly relieved they don't resort to force.

Rule number three, be deaf, dumb, and blind. A must to stay alive. If you don't, you might find yourself in the shark-infested water. I don't know which one was worse.

"You could pay us back faster by spreading those creamy thighs," Deke said with a hungry smile. A small shudder of disgust tried to come over me.

"My offer still stands. Clean slate if I get to pop your cherry," he said while licking his puffy, chapped lips that were stretched into a smile that made his leathery skin more prominent.

I fought another shudder, and I almost lost the battle with that one. I also tasted a hint of bile.

"Thanks, but I like my job," I tell him with my fake as fuck apologetic smile. I really wanted to give him the finger, slap his face, and tell him to fuck off. The man was old and disgusting.

My shoulders sagged slightly as my shift ended. I needed something strong. A few drinks to clear away my fear and disgust that I felt. I also needed a hot shower to wash away the stench of the bar and the feel of their touches.

Another night, only eighteen hundred twenty-nine more to go. The reminder was both a relief and a crushing weight.

Chapter 2
Zane
Earlier That Night...

Lifting the beer to my lips, I looked around the bar now that Sal's gone. Fuck. Sal made a fucking mistake joining up with the cartel and crossing our mother chapter. Reyes, the mother chapter's president, had to send in Gunner.

The shit hit the fan with Reyes girl. Then things really went up shit's creek, and here we are. I was now the new president, a job I didn't want.

I needed someone to go into Bloody Saints smaller chapter and check shit out. This was per the request of the larger mother chapter.

I couldn't send in another brother; this shit was damn near suicidal. It was like playing Russian roulette.

Everyone disagreed with my choice, but in the end, it was mine to make.

The cool, bitter liquid slid into my mouth and down my throat. I needed a moment of freedom before I had to hand over my colors and hit the road.

The plan was to walk into the bar that they owned and pretend to be nothing more than a biker. Someone who knows nothing.

"Fuck, man, I don't envy you," Topher slaps me on the shoulder as he climbs onto the bar stool beside me.

"I fucking hate having to give up my cut," I growled.

He just smiled, the fucker. Shaking my head, I turned back to my beer.

"Send someone else," he said.

"Who? You?" I asked.

He glared at me.

"You would, you fucking asshole," Topher growled.

He's right if I were going to send anyone it would be him. The thought brought a smile to my face.

"I need to go," I tell him.

Sighing, I lift my sorry ass off the bar stool. This shit was going to be a fucking nightmare. We had a lot riding on this deal with the Bloody Saints. They needed us to infiltrate their wayward children, so to speak. That way they could clean house and we, the Grimm Brothers, needed to end this fucking war between us.

Chapter 3
Tori

Earlier That Night...

I wanted something different for my little sister and me. Sometimes I questioned whether staying was smart or if running would be better.

I've had my fill of motorcycle clubs, that's for fucking sure. The nasty things they say and do invokes this horrible feeling. I shudder at the memories of everything that I've seen. I try to push those memories back down to the gates of hell that I've shoved them in.

The buzzing in my pocket had my heart freezing and my lungs deflating. My sister knew not to call me unless it was an emergency. She was eighteen, and I was feeling old at twenty. But she was all that I had, and I was all she had. Fuck you, dad!

Glancing around I took in the few people scattered around the bar. No one was watching me as they were all watching Cherry. Cherry got her name because of her perfect from the bottle cherry red hair.

She swayed as she moved around the room doing gods knows what. It wasn't like she tended bar or waited tables. No, she was one of the "deserts." I like to think of them as club friendlies, as she was friendly with all the men in the room. And in ways that I never want to be.

Looking towards the dark empty hallway, I debated the safety of heading in that direction. I knew Deke was back there, and I made it a personal mission to never be alone with him. I also never used the bathroom here.

The buzzing stopped only to start back up again. Gnawing on my lower lip, I debated what I was about to do. My eyes glanced towards the entrance thinking maybe I could sneak out front. No, they would lose their shit if I walked out of this bar before my shift ended.

Shoulders slumping, I walked quickly to the dark tunnel they call a hallway. Pulling my phone out, I swipe to the right to answer her call.

"This better be life or death," I whispered into the phone.

"He's here again," she mumbled into the phone.

My hand tightened on the plastic device as my stomach plummeted. Oh, mother fucking god. This can't be happening.

"Is the door locked?" I asked her.

"Yes," she whispered.

"Where are you?" I demanded.

"In the closet," she whispered again. This time I could hear fabric shifting.

"Is the bedroom door locked?" I asked her as panic and worry warred inside of me.

"Yes," My sister replied in a rush.

"Listen to me. Keep your phone on you. Call the bar, call the fucking cops, but do not, I repeat, do not let that fucker in," I growled.

"I won't," she mumbled quietly.

Some of the panic that I heard in her voice earlier was missing.

"I put three more deadbolts on yesterday," I reminded her.

That made six altogether.

"And a kick plate," I told her quietly.

The frame would have to break for him to get the door open. Why the fuck did my sister date that piece of shit? I thought about asking the club for help, but I already owed them more then I should.

I feared what payment the club would want if I asked for help. I assume it would be me on my back as they took me one after another. My whole body shuddered in disgust.

"Brittany, listen to me. You will be okay. I will be home in two hours. Can you hold on that long?" I asked her gently.

"Ok," she tells me, her voice getting a firmer edge to it.

What I wouldn't give to take this fear, uncertainty, and pain away.

"I'm sorry," she tells me sadly.

"This is not your fault. That fucker is sick," I tell her. There is no doubt in my voice. I want her to understand no matter how many times I have to tell her. This isn't her fault.

Ronald was crazy. Sure, he was smooth when they started dating six months ago. He was all gentlemanly and so generous. Then he started to get a little possessive and not in a sweet I love you, kind of way.

He started monitoring her calls. Pushing her friends out of the picture. Going as far as to put his hands on my ass. My jaw clenched at the reminder.

I wanted to go to the police the first time he broke into our apartment and stole half our underwear. But the club told me from the very beginning no cops… ever. No matter what.

"I love you," I tell her. "We're going to get through this, I promise."

"I love you, too," Brittany tells me.

I could tell she wasn't so sure about getting through this. I wish I could move, but I was only getting half my wages and half my tips. It was barely enough to put food on the table and keep the bills paid. I fucking hated the dreaded disconnection notice. I've seen too many.

Putting the phone back into my pocket I headed back into the main room, but before I made it all the way to safety, well as safe as it can get, a meaty hand grabbed my shoulder.

Hot breath brushed my ear. Another shudder of disgust.

"Tori," Deke whispered.

"Hey, Deke," I say casually. Almost like we were friends, and the weather was warm and beautiful. Really anything but what was really happening in my chest. My heart pinched, and my body tensed. Oh, god, was I going to get away?

"Where are you going, sweets?" he asked.

"Oh, you know, had to go to the bathroom, that time of the month," I told him.

His hand released me, and I stumbled slightly. Shit, even if it was a lie, I was thankful it dissuaded him from what I was sure he planned on doing.

His silence was my cue to leave, and I took it and ran with it. Well, I almost literally ran with it. I shifted and moved quickly like a nice speed walk. You know when you want to run but don't? Yeah, like that.

Chapter 4
Tori

Now

I felt the breeze as soon as the door opened. It ruffled my hair and sent a chill down my spine. For a moment I contemplated who would be stupid enough to walk into a biker bar. Not just any bar, but the Bloody Saints MC's bar. The assholes were crazy.

I knew for a fact the bikers were all out back. I had watched Cherry, and a few other girls giggle their way down the hallway. They were getting little ass slaps as they went.

My toes were stretched to their limit as I wiped down the wooden tavern table. My breasts pressed firmly against the damp surface. I knew whoever just came in, was getting a nice good look at my ass as it all but fell out of my jean shorts. They reminded me of my small skimpy boy short underwear that I favored.

I felt eyes on me, and for a moment I feared that one of the brothers had come back from the party in the other room. That room was off limits to everyone else. You only went in there to fuck, plain and simple. The moment you crossed over the threshold that was your approval for whatever they wanted. Words no longer mattered.

A small shudder went through me. I learned about the room on the second night that I worked here. A few girls looking for a good time found out the hard way that once they went in that room, the word 'no' fell on deaf ears.

I save as many as I can from making that mistake. As of now, most of the girls who venture back there want what's offered. I have yet to be caught as I would discreetly tell the new girls that they didn't want what was being offered. Some left others didn't.

Guilt still gnawed at me. The looks on the girl's faces who didn't take my warning ate at my insides like an infestation. Especially at the tears, bruises, and ripped clothing. My head hung a little, and my shoulders went to my ears. I wanted to disappear.

I tried to remember why I was doing this. Remembering what was at stake. I can't save all the girls, but I can save my sister and as many as I can.

I spelled it out for them and told them what would happen. The guilt shouldn't be so bad, they chose their fate. Tears pricked my eyes, and I swallowed hard as I fought myself.

Get it together. Get this place clean and get home to your sister. Who thankfully hasn't called back. That meant that Ronald was gone.

I moved around the table to get more coverage, and I lifted my eyes and met striking amber. Something in me screamed to save him.

My feet moved, and I all but ran to the man. His blond hair was like a halo. He looked like a Greek god with an abundance of muscle and sinfully dark tattoos.

"Listen to me, you need to get out of here," I begged him. My eyes pleading.

His eyes narrowed, but he said nothing. His eyes questioned, why the fuck should I do that?

"This is a biker bar. These guys will literally kill you if you're not careful," I tell him slowly. Hoping the words would sink in deep. I couldn't help glancing over my shoulder hoping the club stayed back there.

Again, he said nothing just raised an eyebrow. A silent challenge. My heart beat faster as his eyes darkened slightly. A frown tugged on his full lips.

"Shouldn't you want the service?" His deep voice washed over me, and I gave an involuntary shiver. Something deep inside me clenched. What the fuck?

"You're not listening to me. They. Will. Kill. You." I emphasized every word.

"Listen darlin' I've been riding for hours, and I need a cold beer and some downtime," he tells me quietly.

Shit! He couldn't stay here. His presence was going to cause a lot of trouble. For both him and me.

"Look, this isn't just you on the line here. This is my life too," I tell him as my tone hardened a little.

"Beer, whatever local you have on tap," he replied.

He wasn't leaving without his beer. Giving a nervous look over my shoulder, I bit my lip before turning back to the good-looking guy. For my sanity, please try not to cry.

"One beer and then you'll leave?" I asked him desperately.

I wanted to beg him to just go. Hell, I would offer him a cup to go if it wasn't both illegal and if we had one.

"Sure," he tells me while nodding his head.

I scurry over to the bar. My feet were sticking to the floor, and I grimaced with every step. Grabbing a semi-clean glass, I poured him some Shipyard.

"How long have you been working here?" He asked, his voice was low and sinful.

I bet that tone had panties damping and spontaneously combusting all the time.

"Too long," I tell him with a forced smile.

"Why don't you quit?" He asked, his tone curious.

"Don't have a choice," I tell him with a careless shrug.

It was the truth. I was trapped here in this shitty place watching horrible things happen every day while fighting off the advances of these nasty assholes.

"Huh?" He replied.

"Look, you need to go," I tell him while glancing in the direction of the dark hallway from hell.

"I'm drinking, remember?" He asked with a light laugh.

"Drink faster," I tell him firmly.

"Some bartender you are," he said with a smile.

"This place is not safe. It would be best if you went and don't look back. Trust me I'm doing you a favor," I tell the good-looking guy harshly.

"Sounds like you need to leave too," he tells me with a raised eyebrow.

"Again, I can't. But you can, please," I beg him silently.

I could hear the moans and laughter getting louder, and I shuddered. Tonight, everyone in the room was there of their own free will. All of them knew what to expect. I knew I wouldn't see any tears come morning. It was almost enough to have my shoulders slumping in relief, and I probably would have if this man would take the hint and run for his life.

"What's your name sweetheart?" He asked me.

"Tori," I tell him as I rub down the bar top.

I was almost done, and then I could go home for a few hours. I would need to be back in the morning to clean the backroom when everyone was gone. It was the only time it was safe to be back there.

"Tell me a little about this place," he said it nicely, but I got the undertones that it wasn't optional.

I eyed him again. Was he one of them? A biker? My eyes roamed over his body looking for any hint that I hadn't stepped into deeper shit.

"It's owned by the Bloody Saints MC," I tell him as I lean over the bar dropping my voice. As I got closer to his face, I said, "These guys don't fuck around. I'm literally begging you to get out of here and save yourself."

His lips twisted into a small smile like he found what I said funny. Like he thought I was joking. Shit, I wish I was joking.

My phone buzzed in my pocket, and my eyes closed briefly. Pulling away from the good-looking guy, I reached into my pocket. My eyes looked at the screen before looking down the hallway. The man watched me as he sipped his beer.

I swallowed, and answered the phone and prayed she's not calling because Ronald got inside.

"He's back," she cried.

"Is he inside?" I asked trying to fight down my panic and keep my voice low so the man watching me couldn't hear.

"No, but I'm not sure how long before he will be," she tells me through a deep chest rattling sob.

"Listen to me Brit. I need you to stay calm, okay? I'll be there in maybe twenty minutes," I tell her keeping my voice strong when all I wanted to do was rip at my hair and scream.

"Okay," she whispered between her rattling sobs.

Disconnecting the phone, I looked at the stranger. He needed to go so I could.

"I need you to leave," I tell him coldly.

"Listen, sweetheart…" he started.

"No, you listen. I need you to leave because I need to leave," I tell him as I reached for my purse.

He was studying me, and I fought to keep my face neutral. I didn't have time for his shit. I had another crazy prick to deal with.

"Just go, okay?" I tell him, my voice hardening as I remembered my sister's panicked cries.

Without a word, he stood up dropping three twenties onto the bar and walked away. I wanted to tell him it was too much, but instead, I took thirty-five out of my pocket and put it in the cash box with my name on it. I then slipped the sixty into my pocket.

I wished this night was over, and I wished that I had gotten his number. It was foolish of me, but I had this feeling that he seemed important to me. Shaking my head, I rushed out the door and to my waiting piece of shit car.

The rust was the new rave, I told my sister as another hole appeared in the fender. There was more rust than color to the car, and the seats were sunk in.

I hated it. I hated what our lives have become, and I hated this club. I also hated my father. As I closed the door and started the car, it clunked and rattled. I cursed them all, including Ronald. Fuck them. They may control my life now, but they didn't own my soul, and someday I would be free.

Made in United States
North Haven, CT
29 March 2025